∞ Untold Press ∞

Book One of the Clanless Series

J. A. Campbell

Senior Year Bites

All Rights Reserved
Copyright © 2014 by J.A. Campbell
Cover Design © 2014 by Sean Hayden
Cover Photo © 2014 by Aleshyn Andrei

First Untold Press Publication / July 2014

All rights Reserved. This book or any portion thereof may not be reproduced or used in any manner whatsoever without the express written permission of the publisher except for the use of brief quotations in a book review.

Names, characters, places, and incidents are the products of the author's imagination and or used fictitiously. Any resemblance to actual events, locales or persons, living or dead, is entirely coincidental.

Published by Untold Press LLC
114 NE Estia Lane
Port St Lucie, FL 34983

www.untoldpress.com

ISBN: 978-0692256077

PRODUCED IN THE UNITED STATES OF AMERICA

10 9 8 7 6 5 4 3 2 1

Dedication

For Mardel. Your support means so much to me.

Acknowledgements

There are so many people to mention that I'm sure I'll forget someone. I have to thank my CP's; Nicole, Shanah, Angela, and Devin O'Branagan. I wouldn't be where I am today without your help. Deidre and Mardel. Your continued support has been so important to me. Mom, thanks for reading my stories.

Thanks to my Irish Sailor for being so understanding of writing time. Julie Particka, thank you for all your help and suggestions, especially with blurbs. Becky, you rock. Thanks! I also couldn't have done this without my awesome editor, Terry. Thank you so much for your help. Any mistakes are, of course, mine. And thank you to Jen and Sean of Untold for reprinting this novel.

This novel started as a dream I had about a girl who got turned into a vampire her senior year of high school. Shanah and I decided to both write a few pages based on that prompt just to see how different they would turn out. I never intended to write a novel out of this idea, but after a few pages I found I couldn't stop and the result is what you are about to read. It's been a great journey and I hope you enjoy reading it as much as I enjoyed writing it.

Chapter 1

I had plans for my last year of high school. I was going to find a boyfriend, go to a few dances, and though I hadn't told my mom yet, take some beginning paramedic courses in the spring. I wasn't entirely sure what I wanted to do with my life–wasn't that what college was for? I liked the idea of being a hero, like my dad, and saving lives every day. That had been the plan anyway, but a sleepover and a late-night dare had changed everything.

A lot.

"Megan, time for school," Mom called up the stairs.

I peeked out the window, squinting at the sunlight glinting off the windshield of my Jeep. It was too damn sunny for me to get from my house to the Jeep without third degree burns–or worse.

"Honey?"

My newly sensitive ears could hear the soft brush of her socks on the carpet as she walked up the stairs. I crawled back into bed and did my best to look tired and sick. It wasn't hard with my pale skin, and I hadn't been eating well. If I didn't let her get a good look at me, she might buy that I had a cold or something. Another thought tickled at the back of my mind. I could make her think I was sick. I shoved the thought away in disgust. I wasn't going to use mind control on someone I loved.

The door creaked open and Mom walked in. My heart would have been racing–if it still could.

"Megan?" Mom's voice sounded full of concern.

I groaned and pulled the covers down off my head. "Mmmm?"

"It's time for school. You didn't come down for breakfast." Her flat tone covered her worry with annoyance.

"I don't feel well."

"Honey…."

"I don't." I tried to make myself sound hoarse.

"You've been eating so poorly. Try to eat, and then go to school. I'll write a note for you."

I faked a cough.

Mom sighed. "You've been sick so much recently. Maybe you should go to the doctor."

"No, it's just a cold." I hadn't been "sick" that much. We rarely saw the sun this time of year. As long as I wore sunglasses, a hat, and long sleeves, I didn't burn. It was simply really uncomfortable. I felt horrible for the deception, but what could I do?

"It's beautiful outside for a change. Go outside and get some fresh air."

I panicked at the thought. "No, I just want to sleep." And I did. So very much.

It was hard enough to be awake at all on cloudy days; sunny ones were pure torture.

"Meg."

My stomach sank at the worry in Mom's voice, but I couldn't tell her what was wrong. Not only wouldn't she understand, but I didn't want to end up in the freaking loony bin when I claimed I was something that didn't really exist.

"All right, honey. Sleep well. I'll call in sick for you."

"Thanks." I mentally shrank away from her concern and fought tears of frustration. I didn't want my life to be full of lies, which put distance between us. We had to take care of each other, but I could only hide from her.

She shut my door and left, quiet footsteps strangely loud in my ears. I sighed and pulled the blanket over my head again.

My life changed several weeks earlier at my best friend's ill-fated birthday party. Well, ill-fated for me, anyway. Steph had a great time.

Truth or dare, a stupid game everyone I knew played at least once in their lives. Afraid of the truth, I had chosen the dare–spend the rest of the night in the graveyard near Steph's house. Easy enough, right? Well, it had been up until the point where I was attacked and killed. It wasn't something you normally walked away from, but for better or for worse, I had.

Vampires were in books, movies, and on TV, but I'd never believed they were real. Still, it hadn't been hard to figure out what had happened to me. Dealing with it was another story. It had taken several almost disastrous mishaps–going for a walk in the bright sunshine had been particularly painful–to convince me. Now, the cloudy New England days that had been the bane of my existence provided my only semblance of a normal life.

Predictably, I felt better once night fell. I waited until my mom had been asleep for a while before I dressed, pulling on the same pair of jeans I'd worn earlier and a sweater over a fresh T-shirt. My hiking boots completed the practical outfit. I liked practical, especially for hunting.

Sliding open my window, I climbed out on the ledge. I crouched there for a moment before ducking to slip through the small opening, inhaling the crisp fall air. I shut my eyes, letting my senses stretch out, getting in tune with the night. No one was around. I couldn't fly, at least not yet, but I could slow my fall, which allowed me to jump lightly to the ground out of a third-floor bedroom window.

I stalked out into the night, ravenous. Unable to resist the hunger, I allowed it to drive me, guide me to prey. Tonight, as with most nights, I headed to the next town over. It was less likely I would run into anyone who knew me.

There were bars in the college town, and bars meant easy prey, even for someone underage. Mind control allowed me to get in, and I wouldn't stand out among the other young patrons.

I started to run, faster in death, or undeath, than anyone alive. My new speed was one of the few advantages to being a vampire, especially since I couldn't take my Jeep. It was more likely I'd get caught if I took it, since Mom would notice its absence if she got up at night.

The ground sped past and trees flashed by; their shadows unable to hide their mysteries from my sharp eyes. The night sounds–laughter here, the snap of a twig over there–and smells assaulted my senses. The extra senses had been the hardest thing to get used to: the extra perception. Well, that and having to drink blood.

Both revolted and enraptured, I pondered what I was about to do, drinking someone's blood, taking away a little bit of their life to sustain my own. I wasn't a killer. I couldn't bring myself to go that far and saw no reason to. The alcohol in their blood didn't affect me, and it did half the work for me. Their intoxicated brains gave my new mind control powers enough of an edge that I could make them forget.

The power made me feel strong and dangerous, but it also sent shivers of terror through me. What if I wasn't strong enough to control it? What would happen?

Loud country music and the reek of stale beer hit me as I flashed my ID at the bouncer, batted my eyes, and tweaked his brain. He nodded and waved me into the crowded bar. I pushed into the tightly packed mass of humanity and started hunting for likely prey. A small dance floor took up space in the back, and several giggling women were trying to line dance.

I needed someone male, alone, and drunk for this to work properly in my head. Getting that close to a girl was something I couldn't yet bring myself to do. I spotted a potential subject in the back. He appeared to be in his early twenties, cute, and drinking heavily. I started his way and jumped when a hand touched my shoulder. Some cool huntress of the night I was.

"Yes?" I turned to face the owner of the hand. Young enough to still be in college, he had dark brown hair and eyes, and a nice tan. His winning smile made me feel butterflies all the way down to my toes.

"I've seen you in here before. I'm Gary."

He smiled again, apparently trying to be friendly, but he wasn't drunk enough to suit my needs.

"Hi. I'm Bridget." I didn't want to give him my real name. I did smile back, unable to resist his grin.

Then what he said clicked. He'd seen me in here before. Damn. Sloppy. It looked like I wasn't going to find dinner here tonight.

"Can I buy you a drink?"

I improvised. "No, thanks. I was looking for someone, and she isn't here. I need to get going."

"Maybe next time?"

"Maybe. It was nice to meet you." I headed for the door, watching Gary out of the corner of my eye. He went over to a table with a couple other guys his age and gestured once at me before shrugging.

I put them out of my mind, hunger driving me to the sports bar and my next meal.

The next day turned into a typical cloudy New England day, which meant I had to drag myself out of bed and go to school. I got up after only a few hours of sleep with just enough time to shower. I didn't need a lot of sleep to function, though I never felt rested until the sun set.

"Bye, Mom!" I dashed out the door, running late.

"Bye, Megan. Are you going to eat?" I could hear her hurrying from the kitchen.

"No time. I'll get something at school. I'm late."

I threw my Jeep into reverse and backed out of the driveway before Mom could say anything else. She watched me from the doorway, frowning.

Guilt stabbed me at the endless deception, but what else could I do?

I suffered through my classes in silence. The press of people around me, the coppery smell of blood underlying the odor of deodorant, perfume, and sweat, and my general low-level hunger, made it uncomfortable for me to be around my fellow students. The hunger I could get used to, but I didn't believe I'd ever get over thinking of my classmates as food.

Finally, the lunch bell rang and I picked a corner to hide in. Unfortunately, my friends found me.

"Meg, you've been avoiding us for weeks. What's going on?" Steph sat down next to me.

I inhaled her light perfume. The scent did nothing to cover the smell of the blood flowing in her veins. I could hear her heartbeat, slightly elevated from the walk up the stairs. I wrenched my thoughts away from her blood and stared at the ground in front of me. This was one of the reasons I avoided Steph and Ann. I didn't like my reaction to them. They were my friends, not some nameless guy in a bar. I had a hard enough time with that. I would never hurt them, but the desire was still there.

Ann sat down on the other side of me, finishing her lunch.

A group of cheerleaders flounced by, giggling over the latest gossip. I caught a hint of longing from Ann–her scent changed, and after a moment, I knew what it meant. She'd never be a cheerleader with her plump 5'2" frame. The strong feelings I sensed from her surprised me. I knew she wanted to be popular, but I hadn't felt her desire before. I fidgeted, uncomfortable with the new insight I had into Ann's feelings, but I was intrigued, too.

Curious, I shifted my focus to Steph. She also watched the cheerleaders giggle their way across the commons, but I smelled her contempt. In contrast to Ann, Steph was tall and athletic, with stylish shoulder-length, strawberry blonde hair, stunning blue eyes, and pale skin with a light dusting of freckles across her nose. She could have been a cheerleader but had no desire to hang with them. I knew Ann felt plain next to Steph, but then again, so did I.

I was somewhere in the middle, not tall, not short, with unremarkable brown hair and unremarkable brown eyes. It was fine with me; I didn't need to be noticed. I had been cultivating a friendship with a guy in my math class. He'd even asked me out–right before Steph's party. Canceling the date had sucked, but I couldn't think of anything else to do. I pushed away my anger and frustration and tried to focus on Steph.

"Meg?" Steph said again when I didn't answer her question.

"Huh? Sorry. I've...been feeling sick. Not social today, I guess."

"You look pale. Your mom called the other day and said you hadn't been eating well."

They had no idea. I shrugged.

"Want to have a sleepover this weekend?" Ann asked. "We have not had much time to hang out since Steph's party."

I almost laughed. "Yeah, maybe."

"Cool."

"Did you hear what happened last night?" Ann whispered with a small grin on her face.

"What?" A trill of fear ran down my spine. I knew a few things that had happened last night I didn't want her to know about.

"No, what?" Steph leaned forward slightly, interested in the gossip.

"I guess Derek had a fake ID. He and some friends were at the sports bar watching the game. Well, that was their excuse to their parents anyway. Derek had a lot to drink and left with some girl. Only, he cannot really remember what happened."

I clenched my fists. I had gone to the sports bar and left with some guy. I had thought he'd been alone, but maybe not.

"Yeah, he ended up having to go to the hospital, drank too much and kept babbling about something following him."

Steph gave me a concerned look. "How'd you find out?" She looked at Ann.

"His brother told me in first period." Ann shook her head, but she didn't seem terribly concerned about Derek.

"Is he okay?" I clenched my teeth.

"Yeah, why? He just needed an IV for a while."

I took a deep breath. "Good." What if it had been him? What if he had remembered more than his brother said? I still wasn't very good at my mind control. Shit. What if he saw me and recognized me? I didn't know what to do.

Ann gave me a concerned look before smiling brightly again, glad to be the bearer of interesting news.

Steph turned to me after an extended silence. "So, what's really up?"

"What?" The sudden change in subject confused me, breaking through my mini-panic session.

"Something's obviously wrong with you, Meg. What's up?"

They were my best friends, but how could I tell them? I was saved by the bell, as it were, its loud klaxon ring piercing my skull.

"Gotta go to class."

"Yeah, see ya. I'll call you." Steph stood.

"Okay. Later, guys."

I joined the throng of students hurrying to class, grateful to delay the inevitable questioning a bit longer. I had no idea what to do about Derek. And what did his brother mean about being followed? I hadn't followed him. I'd gone home. I fought the sick feeling in my stomach and tried to focus on getting through my day.

Chapter 2

Another night, another hunt. I jogged along the road, slowly this time, trying to take in more of the nighttime, expanding my senses, letting the currents flow through me.

Muffled feminine screams and a muttered curse shattered the quiet rhythm of the night and startled me, sending fear coursing through my body. I wanted to flee, to hide, but my feet were rooted to the ground, another instinct warring with my fear. This was my hunting ground, damn it, and they weren't going to ruin my territory.

My feet started forward, as if on their own accord. A soft growl escaped my lips.

My senses, already keen, sharpened beyond the range I thought possible. My brain processed every sound, every scent, and a four-dimensional picture of everything around me formed in my head–including the two people struggling by the side of the road up ahead.

"Mine," I muttered and sprinted forward.

A young man struggled with a younger female, trying to throw her to the ground. I smelled alcohol and thought both might be drunk. The woman screamed again, trying to shake the man's hand from her mouth while he pulled at her clothing.

"Hey!" I skidded to a halt.

"Help!" Fear made the woman's voice shrill. She jerked away from the boy, trying to break his hold on her hand.

"Get out of here. This ain't none of your business."

"Isn't any," I corrected, stalling while I tried to figure out what to do.

"What?"

"Isn't any. 'Ain't none' is poor grammar."

"Heh." The boy laughed and finally managed to shove the girl to the ground.

She moaned and lay there, obviously disoriented. I smelled blood and wondered if she'd hurt herself. I wished she would get up and run.

The boy, probably college age, turned and looked at me.

"Well, now…you're cute." He walked toward me, leering.

My anger at his trespass overrode my desire to run. I growled. The guy laughed again and lunged at me when he got close. I let him touch me, just long enough to grab his arm. I twisted him around and threw him on the ground, his skull connecting with a sickening thud against the asphalt. He stopped moving, but he wasn't dead. I heard his heart still beating strongly, tasted the blood flowing just under the surface of his skin, and smelled it where it leaked out of his skull.

I didn't want to touch the disgusting creature, but I bent over him anyway and tilted his head back. The smell of blood forced my lips to his neck. My teeth broke his skin; hot blood rushed into my mouth. I drank my fill, almost killing my prey. He would be in bad shape for a while, but I couldn't bring myself to care after what he was going to do to the girl.

Satisfied, I leaned back and looked around. The world faded back to its normal vibrancy. The girl still lay moaning in the dirt.

She disgusted me, laying there, waiting for rescue.

My irrational reaction surprised me. Obviously hurt, she lay there with her eyes open but unfocused. I glanced around. Her purse had fallen a short distance away, her cell phone lying next to it. Carefully, using my shirt to touch the phone, I dialed 911.

The voice on the other end of the line crackled through the speaker. "911. What is the address of your emergency?"

I hesitated, not sure what to say.

"911. What–?"

I cut the call-taker off. "I'm out on Hallow Lane, on the south side of the road. There's this girl on the ground and a guy unconscious in the street. I'm about a half a mile from town." I dropped the phone, hoping that was enough information, or that they could somehow trace the call.

Emergency vehicles, sirens blaring, sped past me as I headed into town from the heavily wooded stretch between the college and the bars. I stuck to the woods until I made it back to the row of stately Cape Cod homes lining the road on their big lots. I'd always wanted to live in the antique houses, with their inviting front porches and gleaming white shutters. Unfortunately, a fireman didn't make much money, and a fireman's widow certainly couldn't afford one.

I turned off of Hallow Lane and onto Stewart Drive, away from the big houses and into the less-expensive suburbs. The tri-levels and occasional two and three-story homes were nice, but most showed their age. They were kind of like stuffy old ladies, beyond their prime but still proud. I passed the house with the amazing rose garden and turned onto my street. My neighborhood was quiet. The streetlights sent soft pools of yellow into the darkness. I avoided them, feeling like I belonged in the darkness. No light should illuminate the monster I had become.

What I'd done didn't sink in until later in the evening. I lay in bed, reading a book for school and pretending to be asleep should Mom get the urge to check on me, when my hands started to shake. I had almost killed someone–at the very least, seriously injured him–and it had been no harder than taking a breath. Of course, I had probably saved the girl from some severe trauma, but still….

I didn't sleep at all. At school the next day I found myself thinking about the guy I had nearly killed.

It distracted me through the morning, making it easier to stay awake, but harder to focus on classes. Math class wasn't too bad, but Mr. Henderson almost kept me after French class when he noticed me staring at a blank notebook page instead of the assignment.

By lunch break, I thought I had come to terms with what I had done. I'd saved the girl without murdering the guy. What disturbed me most was that I really had wanted to kill him. He'd made me very angry, poaching in my territory. Of course, I wondered when that area had become "my territory," but whatever. I had done what I needed to do, and I would have to deal, because I certainly couldn't undo it.

"Meg!" Steph sat down next to me halfway through the lunch hour.

"Hey."

"Did you hear what happened last night?"

"Uh, no?"

"Yeah, one of the cheerleaders, the one who is dating the college boy? She went to a party and got really trashed. He took her out in the woods, and well, it would have been really bad, but some other chick came along and rescued her. Knocked out her boyfriend–I hope he's an ex now." Steph laughed. "Then she called 911 and left the scene. Apparently we have our own superhero looking out for dumb cheerleaders."

A chill coursed through me.

"Megan?"

"Huh?" I jerked my thoughts back to the present.

"What's wrong?"

"Oh, I'm just surprised that could happen to someone I know. Weird." I tried to keep the tension knotting my shoulders out of my voice.

"Yeah, weird. I didn't know you knew any of the cheerleaders."

"Oh, no. I meant someone from my school. I don't know any of the cheerleaders."

"Right. Well, anyway, I wanted to see if you had heard. Where's Ann?"

"I don't know. Haven't seen her since yesterday."

"Hmm. Well. Do you want to come over to my house after school?"

"Uhh, sure. I'll have to check with Mom, but yeah." I got up from the floor and headed to my locker.

Steph followed. "Okay, give her a call. Let me know."

"I'll call her now." I pulled out my phone. Going to Steph's house would make it harder to avoid her questions, but it would keep me away from Mom.

I tilted my head, cradling the phone with my shoulder while I worked the combination on my locker.

"Hey, Mom."

"Megan? What's wrong?"

"Nothing. I just wanted to see if I can go over to Steph's house after school."

"Sure." She sounded relieved.

"Thanks, Mom. Later."

"Bye, honey. Love you."

"Love you, too." I shut my phone. "I can come." I shoved it in my pocket and grabbed my afternoon books.

"Good. Want to give me a ride?" Steph shifted her backpack to a more comfortable position.

The bell rang, and I inched away from her.

"I'll meet you by the door then. Later." Steph headed off to her next class.

"Later." My next torture session was English. Most people liked English. I liked math.

Something Steph had said followed me into class though. She'd said a superhero had saved the cheerleader. I wanted to be a hero. My dad had been a hero, saving lives until a burning building had collapsed on him. Maybe…no. I pushed the thought away. I was a monster. I tried to focus on the teacher, droning away about the reading assignment.

Monster.

My stomach sank as I stared outside. The setting sun hung low in the sky, bathing the parking lot with a warm glow. It looked bright enough to be painful, bright enough for me to not want to go out in it. I shivered and stepped back into the shadows to wait for Steph.

"Hi, Meg." Steph joined me.

"Uh, hi."

"Ann should be here soon."

"Uh, great. Umm, can we hang out in the library for a little while?"

"Library?"

I glanced outside again. The sun glared back at me, taunting me with its slow decent.

"Hi, guys," Ann said as she came up behind us.

"So, Megan wants to hang out in the library."

I glanced at Steph, surprised at the suspicion in her voice.

"Oh, come on. It is the weekend. Can we just go home?"

Steph ignored Ann. "How long?"

"Um…." I glanced outside again, stepping away from the press of students anxious to get home jostling past us.

"Megan, what's going on?"

"I just need half an hour."

"Meg, even your Mom has noticed that you are avoiding the sunlight."

I froze, instinct telling me to run and hide, or kill the threat. I clenched my fists, fighting the urge to sink into the shadows or fight.

"Meg?" Steph noticed my reaction.

I shook my head. "Let's wait for a few."

"Okay, then we will not have to fight traffic." Ann backed me up but sounded confused.

I wished I had thought of that excuse. I could tell Steph wasn't going to drop the subject.

We turned, heading back into the school, and I stopped cold. Ann ran into my back, but I didn't move. The boy I'd fed from the other night walked down the hall toward me, laughing and chatting with a couple of friends. Damn. I'd hoped I'd been wrong. He must be Derek. I stood frozen, unable to move as he sauntered past.

He glanced at me, and I stopped breathing. His gaze was simply curious, as if he wondered why I blocked traffic. There was no flash of recognition, no accusatory words. He looked tired, a little pale, but otherwise, fine. He pushed past me, continuing his conversation as if I barely existed.

"Meg?"

"Sorry." I pushed my way through the crowd, seeking temporary sanctuary in the library.

Chapter 3

"So," Steph said when we reached the library.

I headed for the back corner where the reference books were. No one ever went back there. I passed the comfy reading chairs, running my hand lightly over the back of one. Two students, the only other occupants, were giggling on the far side of the small room.

"What?" Apparently the library wasn't going to be the sanctuary I had hoped for.

"What's up, Meg?" Steph leaned against a bookshelf.

"Nothing." I folded my arms and hugged myself.

"We're your best friends, right?"

"Yes."

"That means you can trust us, right?" Steph put her hands on her hips, as if daring me to argue with her.

"I need to find a book." I walked away before she could protest and buried myself in the stacks, trying to ignore Steph and Ann's conversation about me and my bizarre behavior. Ann even suggested I might be on drugs. I laughed quietly, even though I wanted to cry.

We finally ventured into the parking lot after most of the crowd had left. It was still too bright out, and my skin tingled despite the long sleeves I wore. I muttered curses at the sun until I could hide in the relative shade of my Jeep.

Steph and Ann caught up with me and gave me concerned looks. I guess I had been running....

The Jeep rumbled to life, and I headed out of the parking lot toward Steph's place, trying not to speed. The sun was almost down, but we were heading west. Every time we broke out of the shade, I struggled not to jerk us off the road.

The sun sank below the horizon by the time we reached Steph's, and my driving had obviously improved, because the white-knuckled grips my friends had on the roll bars had relaxed. I sighed, just grateful it was late fall and the sun went down earlier. I didn't know what I would do this summer.

I parked at the curb in front of Steph's Cape Cod-style house.

"You know, normally you're a really good driver." Steph leapt out of the Jeep.

I shrugged. Both Steph and Ann were pale, their eyes wide. I could smell their fear.

"All right. Inside, hot chocolate to warm us up, then Ann and I want to know what's going on."

"Uh."

"Come on."

Steph led us into her empty home. We always came to Steph's house, because she had no siblings and both her parents worked until six. Ann and I sat around the antique oak table while Steph made hot chocolate. I wasn't sure how to talk my way out of that part of our hang-out ritual, so I kept my mouth shut and waited for her to finish, nervously tracing the wood grain with my fingers.

Steph set a mug down in front of me and slid another to Ann before joining us.

She took a sip and looked at me expectantly. I wilted under her gaze and fought the urge to run.

"So, are you going to tell us what's going on?" Steph stared at me when I remained silent.

I shrugged and fidgeted, avoiding her gaze. Parental grilling I could handle, but the combined stares of my two best friends were too much.

Finally, I caved. What else could I do?

"Let me tell you a story." I didn't know how else to do this. I couldn't get myself to come out and say it.

"Okay." Steph sounded a little confused, but nodded for me to continue.

"It's the middle of the night, and a young girl finds herself alone in a graveyard. It's dark, but not too cold, and the stars are bright in the sky, so it isn't so bad. Our teenager wanders to the edge of the old graveyard and finds a good spot to lie down and stargaze. She's fine for a while, but then she hears some rustling on the southern edge of the graveyard. Curious, she investigates, and when she later tries to remember what she found, she can't. Her friends find her asleep on the ground. It's still before dawn, and though our teen feels weird, she suspects it's from sleeping outside. After several days of increasingly odd urges and a few close calls, our teenager begins to realize something has gone horribly wrong with her. She craves blood, can't stand direct sunlight, and seems to have developed other crazy abilities." I stopped talking.

Steph and Ann looked at me blankly, obviously not getting my story. Then Ann shook her head and looked at me closer. She traded a glance with Steph.

"You. Um…" Ann hesitated then tried again. "Uh, are you serious?"

I looked away, not sure what to say.

"No, really. We want to know what's going on." Steph rested her elbows on the table and folded her hands under her chin.

I fidgeted, shifting uncomfortably in my chair and trying to avoid their stares.

"That's what happened."

"Um, Meg…."

"Ann. That's what happened. I can't help it if the story is crazy. I still don't believe it myself."

"Well," Ann paused, "do you have fangs?"

"Yeah."

"Cool. Let's see."

I clamped my lips together, extremely self-conscious about them. I could sense she didn't believe me and wondered why I'd made up such a bizarre story.

"Oh, come on."

I clenched my jaw and wondered if I could still blush.

"Ann, leave her alone. So how does this work?" Steph's tone was cautious.

"What do you mean?"

"Well, you are claiming that you are a vampire, right?"

I nodded, sure I had a deer-in-the-headlights look.

"That's ridiculous."

I stared at Steph for a moment, flinching at her harsh words. I hadn't expected them to believe me, but the openly hostile tone in her voice stung.

They seemed at a loss for something to say. I sure as hell was. I started squirming when the silence stretched.

"Meg, are you okay?"

"No!" I winced at my outburst. "What about this makes you think I'm okay? I have to drink blood and can't go out into the sunlight. And you don't even believe me. It sucks! How am I supposed to get a tan, let alone a date for prom?" I started to cry, no longer able to contain weeks of hair-pulling frustration, confusion, and a crap load of fear.

They stared at me, stunned. I shoved back from the table and ran outside, throwing myself to the ground under the old climbing tree. I couldn't take their combined stares and disbelief. I wiped my eyes, surprised I could still cry. Then I sniffed, smelling blood. I stared at my hands–covered in blood–and thought I might be going crazy. I hadn't killed anyone, yet I still had blood on my hands. I rubbed my hands on my pants, heedless of the stains, and touched my face. Blood leaked from the corners of my eyes. Horrified, I forced myself to stop crying and scrubbed the blood off my face with my thankfully dark-colored shirt.

I was as composed as I could get when I heard the back door open.

Steph and Ann joined me under the tree.

"I'm sorry, Meg." Steph knelt next to me.

"Yeah, it is just so strange," Ann added.

I fought another crying outburst.

Steph put her arm around me. I let her hug me, appreciating the comfort. I sniffed again, and then inhaled deeply. Steph's familiar scent and the feel of the blood pulsing just below her skin filled me with desire.

I gasped and jerked away from her, suddenly ravenously hungry.

"Meg?" Steph sounded hurt.

"Sorry." I fought tears again. "Sorry, just, uh, don't touch me. I'm, uh…I guess I'm kind of hungry."

Steph blanched, and they both stepped away from me. I didn't blame them.

"So, you are serious then?" Ann glanced at Steph.

"Yeah." I sat down, calmer.

"Weird."

"Yeah," I agreed.

"I guess you're lucky you can go out during the day at all."

"I suppose."

Steph and Ann, braver souls than I, rejoined me under the tree, though they were careful not to touch me.

"Has anyone else been attacked?"

I shrugged. "I don't know. Not that I've run into." I did wonder if I was the only one, and why I had been left.

"That is so horrible." Ann reached for my arm as if she wanted to comfort me, and then hastily pulled her hand back. "What are you going to do now?"

I rested my chin against my knees and sighed. "How the hell should I know?" I stared out into the graveyard that had ruined my life. I shouldn't have been able to see it this late with all the trees surrounding it, but I could—a silent reminder of the horror I was living through.

"This has potential," Steph finally said.

"Uh," I hesitated, not sure I'd heard her right. "Potential to what? Ruin my life?"

"No, to do good." Steph grinned, obviously liking her idea.

Both Ann and I traded glances then gave her our best "you're crazy" looks.

"No, really. You're like super strong and indestructible, right?"

"Uh, I don't know. I can jump really well and run fast." I glanced around, but none of the neighbors were out. It was chilly enough to keep most people inside.

"That's a start. We'll have to figure out what else you can do." Steph clapped her hands together and positively beamed.

"Why?" I was afraid to ask. She was far too excited about her idea, whatever it was.

"To fight crime."

I looked at her, not quite comprehending what she had said.

"What?" Ann stared at Steph.

"You have superpowers now. That's what the strong do–protect the weak. You'll fight crime, and we will be your sidekicks. Whoever did this to you is still out there, and who knows what else exists. We need to protect people!"

"Uh…what?" I still wasn't quite sure I understood her, although her words resonated with the idea I'd pushed away earlier. I wanted to be a hero. Maybe she was right. The jealousy I sensed from Ann surprised me. The emotion curled around her, souring her scent. I couldn't be sure what ran through her mind, but I did know that while Steph was thrilled with her idea, Ann and I had a problem.

Chapter 4

I sat at a booth in the back of my favorite bar, pretending to nurse a drink while I people-watched and considered Steph's idea. I wasn't sure I was up to being a superhero. Hell, I wasn't sure I felt up to facing my friends at our sleepover tomorrow. The idea bounced around inside my head. Yeah, I wanted to be a hero, to save lives, but not anything like a superhero. That seemed so much bigger, so much more than riding around in an ambulance. Actually going out to find people in trouble? It wasn't something I imagined I could do and I couldn't quite wrap my mind around the idea. Hopefully she didn't want me to wear a cape.

The bar seemed quiet for a Saturday night, probably because of some event on campus. The lights were dimmed to hide the years of collected grime and damage drunken college students had inflicted on the dark wood. My vampire-enhanced vision could see the nicks and scratches, and the corners that were never quite cleaned well enough. Several TV's played sports games, though the sound was turned down, and country music pounded against my skull. I had several prospects for my, uh, dinner. I just had to wait for them to get drunk enough and see who left first.

So intent on watching my targets getting sloshed two tables over, I didn't notice Gary until his shadow darkened my table.

"Hi, Bridget." Gary leaned against a chair. "It is Bridget, right?"

"Uh, yeah. Gary, right?"

"Yes."

"Hi." I tried to keep the lack of enthusiasm out of my voice, though I swore quietly as one of my potential meals got up and left. I wanted to get this over with, but Gary stood in my way.

"Why do you always come in here alone?"

I shrugged and tried to watch the other guy while seeming to pay attention to Gary. It was difficult for a moment, and then something shifted, like a part of my brain turned on and there he was. Another portion of my brain kept track of my prey and allowed me to focus my eyes on Gary. It felt weird, almost like the four-dimensional picture my mind had created for me when I rescued the cheerleader, only more focused.

"Do you mind if I join you?"

Yes! I wanted to scream at him.

"No. Go ahead." Something about Gary's interest bothered me. It didn't seem like I interested him because I was a girl and he was a guy. It seemed to be something else, though I wasn't sure what. My instincts were screaming at me to run or to kill. I fought for a happy medium–try to figure out what he wanted.

Gary slid into the chair across from me, and I tried to figure out his age. He didn't seem much older than me, though obviously he was at least twenty-one.

"Do you go to the college? I haven't seen you there."

"No, I–" I almost told him I went to Banks High School. "I'm saving money for school." That was true, in a way, though how I would go to college now, I didn't know.

I didn't ask him a return question, hoping he would take the hint. My prey still sat at his table, drinking another whatever and getting more sloshed. Which was fine with me.

The silence stretched for a while, growing uncomfortable.

Gary shifted in his seat while I stared at him, his taste going from inquisitive to nervous, tinged with fear. Gary shifted again, glanced away, and cleared his throat.

I jerked my attention away from Gary's neck. I lost the sense of my intended prey in my distraction and looked over toward his table. Damn. He had left. I managed to hold back a growl.

"So, you seem a little young to be in here." Gary fidgeted.

I had to wrench my gaze away from his neck again. The burning need for blood made my hands shake. I shrugged. "They let me in. I must be old enough."

"Ahh, right."

The bar got more crowded, and unfortunately, no one else came alone.

"So, are you looking for someone?"

"No." I stood abruptly, making Gary jump. "I need to go. It was nice talking to you." I walked away before Gary could recover from his surprise and ask me yet another question.

I took a deep breath of the crisp air once I was outside, reveling in the night.

Its pulses filled me, making my senses sing. A familiar presence left the bar, trailing after me. Damn it.

I did growl then, annoyed and more than ready to harm Gary. I was tempted to take him as my dinner, but I curbed those thoughts and headed out into the street toward the sports bar. I focused the part of my brain I apparently could use to keep track of prey on Gary, using the rest of my senses to watch the night.

Cool air brushed my cheeks. The occasional car sounds from the nearby freeway and Gary's harsh breathing broke the peace. Finally, he slipped out of sight. I ducked down into the underbrush, gathering the shadows around me, hiding in plain sight. Gary, though he looked right at me, walked past.

Instinct screamed at me to hunt and kill, and I wanted to follow Gary but I backed off, trying not to lose my tenuous control.

Gary's emotions altered to confusion, and I grinned. He kept going, and I hurried back to the bar.

I didn't want any of his friends to see me, so I waited outside for someone to leave alone. I waited several long hours, but finally, someone did leave. She was stumbling drunk, and because she was female, I almost disregarded her. I wasn't interested in girls, but my hunger spoke up, saying it didn't matter. I fought with myself for a while, but when it became apparent she was walking back to campus alone, my decision was sealed. I couldn't pass up this prey. My body wouldn't let me.

I slipped through the woods, focusing my attention on my prey as it stumbled along the roadside. Joy of joys, it fell. I almost pounced from the trees, but the grumble of a car engine stopped me, and I crouched down, hoping they wouldn't notice my food along the side of the road.

The headlights of the sedan passed over my quarry, and the car didn't even slow down. Perhaps they hadn't seen it, though I couldn't imagine missing such delicious heat and confusion.

Finally, we were alone. My prey had staggered back to her feet and leaned against a tree. I shivered in anticipation and crept forward. I hesitated, fighting with myself for a second, as I stood behind her. I didn't want to do this, but I couldn't resist the hunger.

Her glassy eyes widened when I stepped in front of her, and she tried to step back, but her alcohol-muddled mind was easy to take over. She stood taller than me, but not by much. I tilted her head back and sank my teeth into her neck. The hot rush of coppery, salty, sweet blood filled me with pleasure. More. I wanted more.

I got myself under control. I didn't want to kill her. Hell, I didn't want to do this at all. At least when I wasn't hungry, I didn't want to. I held the girl as she swayed listlessly, not really alert, unsure what to do with her. A guy I would have left. It would be safe enough in this town. But a girl? I wasn't about to put her in more danger.

Finally, I slung her arm over my shoulder and helped her stumble back toward the college. I pushed Steph's superhero idea out of my head again. I was a monster. I fed on people. There was nothing heroic about me.

I dropped her off near one of the dorms and, disgusted with myself, sprinted home. Coming home always made me nervous, afraid my mom had noticed I was gone. I crouched on the roof, watching, making sure my room was empty before I lifted the window and entered my bedroom.

Chapter 5

I managed to force myself awake later in the afternoon. I stumbled into the bathroom and let the hot shower wash away the stress until I felt almost normal, though I wasn't sure what normal was anymore.

Thoughts that had been nagging me over the last couple of weeks came back again. What did this really mean for me? I was a monster now. What other monsters were out there? Would I run into more vampires? Would I run into the one who created me? That idea filled me with a weird combination of fear and curiosity. I wanted to know why I'd been left to fend for myself. Was that normal? Maybe he hadn't realized I would survive.

Hot water warmed me as I leaned against the shower wall and hugged myself, fighting tears. How could I live like this? And how long would I live? Vampires in legends lived forever, or until someone killed them. Would I? I rubbed at my eyes and put my face under the water, letting it wash away the bloody tears. How could I face living forever if it meant feeding off of humans?

Those thoughts were too permanent, and I didn't have any answers. I didn't even have anyone I could ask. Steph and Ann knew my secret now, but they wouldn't know anything more than I did. I got out of the shower and dried off, managing to get the depression threatening to overwhelm me under some semblance of control.

I dressed, threw some clothes in a bag, and half-heartedly ran a brush through my hair. Then I stumbled downstairs, hardly the graceful huntress of the night. I laughed at myself.

"Good morning, honey." Mom mocked me. There were dark circles under her brown eyes.

"Hi, Mom." I tried to ignore the guilt I felt. I knew I had caused some of her stress.

"Your brother called this morning. He wanted to talk to you, but I couldn't wake you up. He said he'd call back tonight."

"Oh, no." My brother, John, was in the Army over in Afghanistan. I missed him horribly. It was bad enough having Dad gone–he'd been gone for years–but without John, the house felt terribly empty. His ready laugh and smile would be very welcome right now. "Did you tell him to call me at Steph's house?"

Mom nodded.

"Thanks."

I winced at the concern in her eyes. It seemed like she had more lines on her face, too. John being overseas wasn't easy on her, and now I started acting all strange. I suspected she wanted him to try to figure out what was going on. I wasn't sure what I'd tell him–obviously not the truth.

"Sure. Are you leaving now, or do you want to eat first?"

"I'm going now." I lifted my overnight bag and headed for the door.

"All right, honey. I'll see you tomorrow. Be careful."

"Thanks, Mom." I gave her a quick hug before I ran out the door.

"Hey, Steph," I said when she answered the door. "Where's Ann?" I sensed she wasn't here.

"Ann said she'd be by a little later. Apparently she had something to do."

"Really?" I tossed my bag onto the floor as Steph gave me a look. "Well, it just seems odd."

"I know. She's been hanging out with some other people recently."

"Weird."

Steph shrugged. "I thought so. It isn't like I don't think she shouldn't have other friends, but she's been hanging out with them more than me and you. Of course, you've been hiding, too, but that makes some sense."

I gave a halfhearted attempt at a smile. "Yeah, well."

"Anyway, I've been doing some research." Steph gestured to her bed.

I groaned when I saw the library books she had scattered across her fluffy comforter. Bram Stoker's *Dracula* lay amongst several non-fiction titles like *Vampires, Ghosts, and Werewolves*, and a notepad with Steph's messy scribble all over it.

"I mostly wanted the nonfiction stuff, but I figured because Bram Stoker is one of the first vampire writers, maybe he knew something. Besides, you can go out in the sunlight like Dracula. Most vampires can't in the stories."

"Okay."

"So, between *Dracula* and several of these, I have things I want to try. Here, hold this."

I jumped back in alarm when she thrust something large in my face. "What the hell!"

"Okay. No crosses." She tossed the wooden cross on the bed and picked up her notebook.

"What? Uh, wait. You just startled me. I don't think it's actually a problem."

"Oh?" Steph picked the cross back up and tossed it at me.

Catching it, I wondered if anything would happen. I felt–maybe–a mild tingle, but it could have been my poor, abused imagination. I handed it back to Steph. "Nothing."

"Good." She scratched out something. "Okay. I couldn't get any holy water, but here's some garlic. Is it revolting?" She held up a clove of garlic.

I laughed at her. "Umm, it stinks." My eyes started to burn.

"Here."

I accepted the garlic and wondered if I was supposed to burst into flames. I really didn't know much about vampires, so I wasn't sure what should happen. Of course, I hardly thought *Dracula* counted as a good source.

I sneezed.

"Okay. I'm going to guess garlic is mildly irritating." Steph took the clove back and put it in a bag. I felt better almost instantly.

"Joy. Guess I'm going to have to hide out on Italian night at home."

Steph laughed. "Do you know how fast you heal yet?"

"Uh. No."

"Want to find out?"

I stared at the knife she held, horrified. I wasn't going to cut myself.

"Make a small scratch in case you don't heal quickly."

"Um…"

"It'll be okay, Meg."

I gave in. "Sure." I stared in fascination as blood welled up around the cut on my forearm. I slid the sharp knife deeper into my skin.

"Meg! A small cut."

I jerked myself out of my trance and removed the knife from my arm. I resisted the urge to lick my blood off of the knife–for about five seconds–and then I brought the knife to my mouth. The salty tang of blood coated my tongue with bliss.

"Uh, Meg?"

I jerked the knife out of my mouth. "Sorry." I looked down at my arm and watched, fascinated, as the wound closed. I licked the excess blood away from my arm, and within minutes it healed, slowly sealing from the edges until a thin line remained. After a few moments, even the faint scar vanished.

"Damn."

"Cool." Steph grinned at me.

"I think you're insane." I really did. I'd be a lot more freaked out if my best friend suddenly gained the power to heal like that. Her acceptance touched me. It made this a lot easier.

Steph shrugged. "Not much we can do about it, so freaking out isn't going to help. Besides you got, uh, hurt at my birthday party, which makes it partially my fault."

"Ann's here." I was glad she had missed the knife experiment. Ann wasn't nearly as excited about my new condition as Steph was.

Steph looked at me, surprised. "That's handy, too."

"Ycah. I gucss."

I could hear Ann and Steph's mom exchange quick words before Ann came up the stairs. Each footfall sounded like I stood next to her, closer even, like my ear was attached to her foot. It felt weird.

"Hey," I said when she opened the door. I looked at Ann in surprise. She wore a skirt and a nice blouse. I hadn't seen her in a skirt in ages. "What's the occasion?"

Ann blushed and stammered something I couldn't make out. "I felt like dressing up earlier. Anyway, I have clothes to change into."

"You do look nice," Steph added. "Okay, back to the testing."

"What?"

"We're trying to find out Meg's weaknesses and strengths. She can heal really quickly, crosses don't bother her, but garlic does."

Ann glanced at Steph's bed and giggled. "*Dracula*?"

"We had to start somewhere, and it's, well, a classic."

"So is *Frankenstein*."

"Yes, so it is, and if we had to deal with a deranged, pieced-together monster and a mad scientist, I'd have grabbed it."

Ann's smile faded. "Yeah. I guess so. I am going to change."

"What's next?" I asked when Ann left the bedroom.

"Well, I think for everything else we'll wait until we can go outside. I want to see how fast you can run and stuff. Then maybe we can go out patrolling."

"'Patrolling'?" Ann returned to the room.

"What?" I echoed.

"Patrolling. You know, looking for supernatural crime to fight."

"You do realize this is, like, Sleepy Town, USA, not Sunnydale, right? Nothing happens here."

"You got attacked. Maybe if people like us had been out, you'd still be, well, um, human."

I wasn't quite sure what to say to that. I supposed she had a point, but still. I didn't think we were going to find anything. Monster, you're a monster, not a hero. I had to repeat the words to remind myself. No, we wouldn't find anything, and there was no one out there to save.

"We can order pizza and eat it here, that way Meg does not have to pretend not to eat."

I felt both revolted and instantly hungry at the thought of pizza. I loved pizza.

Well, I used to love pizza.

"What's wrong?" Steph asked.

"What?"

"You went all pale, paler, but you look hungry."

I laughed. "Pizza sounds really good and really horrible at the same time." I sighed. "I think I'm going to miss pizza."

"Can you eat food?"

"I don't think so."

"That sucks," Ann said, giving me a sympathetic look.

"Yeah, it does."

She smiled and started to relax a little.

Sitting around while Steph and Ann ate pizza was torture, but I survived. Once they had finished, we went outside.

"Is this really necessary?" I stared at the tree Steph told me to climb. A good climbing tree, we had once spent lots of time in it when we were young, but the boards we'd used to reach the first branch were either rotted or gone.

"Yeah. Just get in the tree."

I studied it, wondering the best way to get to the upper branches. I knew I could jump that high, having done it to get back into my bedroom, but I still felt very self-conscious.

"Come on," Steph said.

I sighed and jumped for thc first branch, easily within reach, caught it, and swung myself up into the tree.

"Happy?"

Steph and Ann stared at me.

"Megan! Phone for you," Steph's dad called out to us.

"Okay," I yelled back and stepped off of the tree branch, landing lightly behind Steph.

"Ahh!" She flinched when I touched her shoulder. "Don't do that."

"Sorry." I smiled. She was the one who wanted to test my powers. Steph gave me a dirty look.

"Come on. It's probably my brother. Can I use the phone in your room?"

"Sure."

"Thanks." I ran up the stairs and grabbed the phone off of its cradle. "Hello?"

"Hey, Meg." My brother's voice came across the line, slightly tinny as if from a great distance.

"Hi, Johnny. How are you?"

"Fine. Mom tells me you've turned into a vampire."

I choked. "What?"

Steph and Ann shot me concerned looks when they entered the room.

"Well, you're avoiding sunlight and not eating. What am I supposed to think?"

"Umm, I don't know. I'm eating. Ask Steph. We had pizza for dinner."

"All right. She is really concerned, though. What's up?"

I looked at Steph, not sure what to say. Steph shrugged. Ann did the same when I shot her a desperate look.

"Nothing. Just not hungry, except for pizza." I laughed. "Maybe I'm a pizza vampire."

"I see." He sounded amused. "Well, I'll tell Mom to watch out for drained pizza around the house."

I smiled. If I could keep him joking, he would help calm Mom down. It was good to hear from John, even if his questions terrified me. I worried about him overseas.

"I love you, John."

"Love you, too, Meg. Be careful."

I laughed. "Me? You're the one getting shot at."

"Naw, I'm not on the front line. Take care of Mom. I have to go now."

Chapter 6

"So, how do we do this?" I asked once we were back outside.

Steph shrugged. "Let's start walking, I guess." She headed away from her house and from the neighborhood. Grateful she didn't go near the graveyard, I did question her sanity when she led us toward the wooded parts of town. Most of the town was surrounded by a thinly wooded buffer which hadn't been cleared for homes.

Ann sighed, and I echoed it, exasperated. This was an idiotic idea.

"We aren't going to find anything," I said. "We aren't superheroes, you know. Stuff like that only happens in TV shows or movies."

Steph arched her eyebrow at me. "Obviously not." I could smell her sarcasm–a bitter flavor on the back of my tongue.

She had a point. People didn't get turned into vampires at slumber parties either.

"How long are we going to do this?" The displeasure in Ann's voice was very obvious.

Steph looked surprised, as if she hadn't considered the question. "Do you mean tonight or in general?"

Ann shook her head. "Never mind. Lead on."

I glanced back and forth between the two, startled by the sharp anger I could sense from Steph and the sour annoyance flavoring Ann's scent. Their feelings set me on edge, and I glanced around the dark night, alert for danger.

Nothing. I couldn't even sense the presence of the sparse wildlife that populated the suburban area. Their absence actually worried me more than my friends' anger. There should be something. I looked around, tuning out everything in my immediate vicinity. The shadows lightened, fading away completely in the open areas, becoming insignificant in the woods. The slight rustle of a few lingering leaves whispered in my ears. The trees creaked and sighed, loud against the still night. I turned my head, peering into the darkness, certain something had scared away the wildlife, but unable to find it. I shivered and narrowed my focus back to my normal perception.

"What?" I asked after I saw the shocked expressions on Steph's and Ann's faces. The sweet scent of fear colored the night.

"Your eyes went completely black. It was freaky." Steph took a deep, calming breath.

Ann nodded, eyes wide. I heard her heart race.

"Huh." Mental note: don't do that around people. "Sorry." I looked down, shoving my hands into my pockets and clenching my jaw.

"It's okay, Meg," Steph said after a moment. "It's just going to take some getting used to."

Ann avoided my gaze. It stung a little, but there wasn't anything I could do about her fear.

"Fine. Let's go then." Some of the tension I felt must have come across in my voice, because Ann flinched.

Steph jogged to catch up when I started walking again. I stopped and waited for her, glancing back at Ann. Ann tasted nervous to me. I wasn't especially hungry, but the scent of fear that trickled off of her was intoxicating. I wrenched my gaze away from her before I could make her more nervous, which would in turn attract my attention more, which would make her worse, which–yeah, vicious cycle. Thinking of my friends as food made me distinctly uncomfortable. Ann finally joined us.

Steph finally asked, "Are you all right?"

"I don't know, but we should go." It felt like something watched me, and the sensation didn't help my discomfort.

We traded looks again before we continued on. Afraid our friendship wouldn't survive the changes, my mood sank even lower. We'd been close for so long I couldn't imagine not having them around, but there were things we'd never do together again. We'd never go swimming on those rare sunny days, or drive with the top down on the Jeep just for fun. Those cheerful thoughts kept me occupied for a while as we walked. I pushed away my sorrow, trying to focus on whatever watched us. I found nothing, but the feeling didn't leave.

"Where are we going?" Ann looked around while we walked.

"Toward the college. It's the only place where anything happens in this town," Steph said.

Steph had a point. That was why I went hunting there, although I wasn't going to share that bit of information.

It surprised me how long it took us to leave the wooded residential areas of our little community and hit the outskirts of the bigger college town. I'd been taking that route recently but at my vampire pace. There were several bars, a few coffee shops, bookshops, and all of the big chain stores.

The area still had a lot of trees, though much had been cleared to make room for parking lots and buildings. We walked along the main road connecting our sleepy New England village to this slightly less sleepy town, as there really wasn't any other way, except trails through the woods. Even Steph wasn't stupid enough to look for trouble there. After a while, the feeling of being watched faded away, and slowly, the normal night sounds started up again.

As we got closer, the loud country music from the bar started to cover the racket from the night insects. I smelled the stale beer and smoke, heard the laughter, shouting, and loud babble from the patrons. My ever-present hunger urged me to leave the humans and go feed. That I already associated bars with food, disturbed me enough to quell my hunger.

Several angry shouts and something breaking caught my attention as we neared The Long Branch, the bar I preferred. I fought the urge to run forward and investigate, unwilling to put my friends in danger. From the way Steph and Ann were calmly walking, scanning the surroundings, I figured they hadn't even heard it.

I stopped at the edge of the parking lot, hiding in the shadows of the trees.

Steph and Ann stopped as well and looked at me, confused.

"Let's wait a minute. Something's wrong."

"Damn it, give me the keys," an angry woman snarled, though I could hear the edge of tears in her voice.

"Listen, bitch, what do you care? You said we were through. Get the fuck out of my way," an equally angry guy slurred.

"I don't give a damn what you do to yourself, asshole, but you could hurt someone else."

"I'm fine."

Something crashed, and several shocked voices cried out. The woman started crying, and a guy stormed out of the bar. Another person spoke quietly about calling the cops, and the sobbing female pleaded against it.

The guy staggered to his car, a beat-up old station wagon, and started the engine.

"What's going on?" Steph whispered.

I winced, her words overly loud to my enhanced hearing. "A fight. She didn't want him to drive; he is anyway."

The station wagon backed out of its parking spot, narrowly missing the cars on either side, and bumping against the fenced smoking area. The gears shuddered as he threw the car into drive. Gravel crunched under the tires as the car slowly turned toward the exit–and us. Rocks flew as the angry drunk slammed on the gas. The wheels fought for purchase before the car jumped forward, still fishtailing.

Everything slowed down until I felt like I had all the time in the world to grab Ann's and Steph's arms and pull them out of its path. I stopped by the fence and watched emotionless as the car plowed into the tree we'd been hiding behind.

Someone shouted, "Meg!"

I staggered as everything sped up to normal speed–shouting, screaming, the horn blaring, and steam hissing from the cracked engine assaulted my ears.

Someone yelled to call for the cops, others for an ambulance. I stood and stared, finally shocked by it all.

"Meg!" Someone shook my shoulder.

I jumped and spun around, crouching, expecting an attack.

Steph backed away, arms out. "Sorry," she whispered, eyes wide. Ann stepped away as well, eyes equally huge.

I took a deep breath, struggling to tune out the chaos around us.

"You guys all right?" I finally managed to ask.

They both nodded, glancing over at the car and back to me. Steph looked over my shoulder, tilting her head slightly.

"Bridget! How in the hell did you do that?"

My breathing quickened, and the urge to run made my legs twitch. Gary's familiar scent penetrated my shock.

"Shit," I whispered.

"Bridget?" Steph gave me a confused look.

I could have killed her then, in the brief instant before I regained my composure. My focus sharpened like it did when I felt threatened. I hurried away from all of them, not wanting to lose control and attack my friend, not wanting to face Gary and his questions, and above all, not wanting to face the fear that made Ann tremble every time she glanced my direction.

"Meg!" Steph called, coming after me.

My instincts shouted at me to run, but I couldn't leave them. They were out here because of me, and I had to make sure they stayed safe. Even Sleepy Town, USA had its dangers.

I stopped at the edge of the woods, away from the chaos of the crash, and away from potential questions from the authorities. Rough bark dug into my shoulder when I leaned against a tree, further anchoring me to reality. Ann and Gary hesitated a few moments longer than Steph, but they weren't far behind her.

"Meg." Steph carefully didn't stand too close.

I appreciated the distance, but I had calmed by the time Ann and Gary caught up. Gary, amazingly enough, kept quiet. I actually liked him a little for it.

"So, Meg, want to introduce me to your friends?" He finally had the nerve to ask after the silence stretched out for several minutes.

He didn't even emphasize my name, simply said it as if he'd always known it.

"Gary, Steph and Ann."

Sirens wailed in the distance, but only I could hear them. "Guys, unless you want to stay and talk to the cops, we should probably get out of here."

"Great. There's this coffee shop within walking distance that will be open a bit longer. Let's go chat," Gary suggested.

I glared at Gary, but Steph and Ann were still shaken and agreed at once. I shrugged, and we hurried into the woods before someone could see us.

"There have been some strange things happening recently, so we thought we should look into it." Steph had perfected her we've-watched-too-much-Buffy speech.

It sounded lame, but at least she didn't give him details about the incident that had sparked her idea.

The strange thing was, Gary didn't seem like he thought this was really dumb. Instead, it seemed like he seriously considered what Steph had to say. He leaned back when she finished, considering us for a moment. His gaze lingered on me, but he had yet to say anything about our previous meetings. He didn't comment when I declined coffee, even though he paid for Steph's and Ann's.

I could feel the curiosity from my friends, and I knew I'd get grilled later, but they refrained for now.

"I have a couple of friends who feel the same way you do. Maybe we should get together next weekend and compare notes."

What?

Steph's eyes lit up, and even Ann seemed relieved that he didn't think we were crazy.

"I think that's an excellent idea." Steph looked at me with a question in her eyes.

I buried my face in my hands and sighed. "Sure, whatever," I muttered.

We made it home late, Steph full of plans and Ann not as sure but not openly hostile to the idea. I couldn't see this going anywhere good, but what the hell. As long as Gary and his friends didn't find out what I was, it couldn't be too bad. That semi-comforting thought lulled me to sleep, and only a persistent shaking woke me the next afternoon.

I bolted upright, preparing to defend myself, teeth bared, snarling.

"Hey!" Steph threw herself backward, tripping over a chair and falling to the floor.

I took deep breaths, trying to calm myself. "I'm sorry," I finally said while Steph lifted herself off the floor.

"It's...okay." The heady aroma of fear wafted off of her skin.

I shuddered and wrenched my gaze away from her neck before she could notice. "What's wrong?" *Besides me?*

Steph took a moment to orient herself before picking something up off the ground and thrusting it at me.

I had enough control by now to not react violently to the paper fluttering in my face, and I took it from her as calmly as I could. The front headline read "College Student Murdered," and underneath, large and in color, I saw a startlingly familiar face, though I remembered the sweet taste of her blood more than her actual features.

What the hell? I hadn't killed her? Had I?

Chapter 7

"Meg, are you okay?"

I stared at the newspaper, my hands shaking, her words not registering.

"Meg?" Steph touched my shoulder.

I jumped and looked up at her.

"Are you okay?"

"Uh, yeah." My voice quavered. I unclenched my hands, the crackle of the newspaper loud and startling. Fear coursed through me, and I wanted to run or kill something, a reaction I barely quelled.

The monster inside me screamed the danger came from Steph. I had to kill her. She was the reason things were spinning out of control. The reason I felt afraid. I took a deep breath and fought with myself. The fear of hurting Steph managed to give me the edge I needed to get a handle on my instincts. I wouldn't be able to live with myself if I hurt my friends.

Had I killed her?

"I'm okay," I finally replied.

She frowned. "Please, Meg. Talk to me."

I shook my head. I couldn't even begin to talk about it.

"Meg, you can trust me."

"I know." I knew I could, but I couldn't talk about it yet.

"I'll let you go back to sleep if you want."

"No, I'm awake now. I should probably get home."

"It's sunny outside."

"Damn."

"Ann went home. You're welcome to stay until the sun sets, of course."

I sighed. "All right." Like I had a choice. I flopped back into my sleeping bag.

"Want to play a game?" Steph asked hesitantly.

"Uh, sure." Anything to distract me until I could get home and think or at least get out alone.

I didn't manage to find time alone until the sun set. Too afraid to hunt, all I could do was toss and turn, the image of the dead girl haunting me.

She'd been alive when I left her. I knew it, but what if she'd died from blood loss later? How could I live with that?

The sky was still black when I finally pulled myself out of my half sleep, enough to get ready for school. At least I would be able to go today. I still didn't know what I would do this summer, or next year, when I had to go to college.

"Megan!" Mom called my name as I dashed down the stairs, trying to make it outside before she made me eat.

"Yeah?" I paused by the door.

"It might snow today. Be careful." She frowned at me. "You look tired."

I shrugged. "I didn't sleep well."

Mom shut her eyes for a minute. "Okay. Be careful. You heard about the murder?" She had her normally neat, shoulder-blade-length hair tied back in a hasty knot at the base of her neck, and the lines on her face seemed deeper. I imagined I could see more gray mixed in with the brown, too.

I fought a tremor of fear. "Yeah." My voice came out in a harsh whisper.

"Be careful, honey, until they catch whoever it is that killed that poor girl. Maybe you could have Stephanie come over here after school until her parents get home."

"That's a good idea, Mom. I'll talk to her about it."

"Bring Ann, too."

"Thanks. I gotta go." I shifted impatiently.

"I love you, honey."

"Love you, too, Mom." I tried to let my voice carry the love I felt for her, because I knew I had been distant recently.

Guilt twisted my stomach as I ran out of the house. I knew she wanted to hug me, but I was afraid she'd notice my low body temperature or my lack of a pulse or something. My skin felt really cold today. And I was hungry. Very, very hungry. The clouds hung heavy in the sky, dark and full of snow. The first flurries fell as I pulled out of the driveway. This storm seemed like it would be a big one.

I let thoughts of the weather distract me from my growing anxiety. It worked until I found Steph and Ann in the cafeteria. We had about a half an hour before homeroom, and I sank to the floor next to them.

Steph and Ann were talking about the murder when I joined them.

"You okay?" Steph asked after she looked up at me.

"Yeah." I tried to make my voice sound normal. By the dubious expression on Steph's face, I didn't succeed.

I considered telling her I was just hungry when a shadow fell over me. I glanced up to see two seniors I didn't know looming over us. I fidgeted, their presence not helping my hunger or my anxiety.

"Mary Ann, what are you doing here?"

I was sure I shared the shocked expression on Steph's face as we both looked at Ann. She actually looked and smelled guilty.

Guilt is a sour smell, a mix of fear, sorrow, and defiance, though I had no idea how I knew. Ann glanced at us quickly before standing.

"I, uh, nothing. Come on."

She walked away without a backward glance. The two girls smirked at us, as if they had won something, before flouncing off after Ann.

"Is it just me or was that really weird?"

"Yeah. That was really weird," I replied. I memorized the two girls, the reek of lavender soap that hung around the dark-haired girl, the coppery scent underlying it. The other girl smelled powder fresh, probably from her deodorant, with a hint of sweat. I suspected she hadn't showered today.

I was really glad I could turn the super smell off, because having to smell everyone all the time would have been really uncomfortable. Of course, I couldn't always control when it turned on.

Damn, now that I'd smelled blood, my hunger made itself known. The two girls were obviously trespassing into my territory and taking their blood–and their lives–seemed, for a moment, a perfectly good idea.

"Meg?"

I took a deep breath and unclenched my hands, trying to control my reaction. Ann wasn't my territory, and if she wanted to go off with other people, that was fine with me. I repeated it to myself until I almost believed it.

"What's wrong?"

"Just hungry," I muttered.

"Oh." Steph's generally neutral feel shifted into fear.

I groaned. "Damn it, I'm fine. Don't do that."

"What?" She sounded confused.

"Nothing." I focused my attention on the ground in front of me. "Mom said you should come home with me after school. She's worried about you alone in the house with a murderer around." Of course, she might be going home with the murderer, but I couldn't tell her that.

Steph took a deep breath and her scent went neutral again. "That's a good idea."

"I was going to ask Ann, but, well, whatever that was about."

Steph nodded. "She has been acting a little odd recently."

"Yeah."

The bell rang for homeroom. I stood and offered Steph a hand. Touching her was a bad idea, the contact tingling up my arm as I pulled her to her feet a bit too hard. She stumbled into me, her familiar smell filling me with desire. I had to jerk myself away before I did something we'd both regret.

"Meg?"

"Sorry." I fought a flush of embarrassment. I definitely wasn't interested in girls, but the hunger didn't care about my preferences, and it told me blood tasted so much better when combined with other things.

"I have to go!" I fled before my thoughts went any further.

The day got steadily worse. A pop quiz in my first class–history–set the tone for the day. I thought I did okay on the quiz, but my ability to focus went downhill rapidly. Being surrounded by warm, beating hearts and the scent of blood was driving me nuts. I quickly realized what a mistake it had been to not feed the night before.

I made it to third period chemistry without jumping a freshman in the hallway and tucked myself into my corner seat, grateful for a hands-on class to occupy my mind. I glanced out the window to distract myself from so many easy snacks and was surprised at how much snow had fallen in the last several hours. My first two classrooms didn't have windows.

Several of the students were wondering if we were going to get sent home, and my teacher kept shooting nervous glances outside. We were used to snow in New England, but even we couldn't drive in several feet of unplowed snow. None of us wanted to get stuck at school.

I finished my lab quickly, knowing if I took too long at it, I'd lose focus. Three titrations didn't take very long. I could see the smallest change in the color of the liquid before anyone else could, so I didn't have to redo any experiments, which helped.

Dawn, the girl who shared the table with me, muttered about wanting to go home. The snow had to be at least a foot deep.

I shoved my books into my backpack. My teacher gave me a weird look when I'd cleaned up so early, but after checking my work and giving me a surprised, "Good job," she'd let me return to my desk. I didn't have anything else to do, except homework, but I wasn't able to focus.

The tinkle of glass and the sharp smell of blood jerked my head around, and I got out of my seat before I could stop myself.

Dawn glanced at me, eyebrows arched before turning hastily away.

I ignored her, focused on the blood I craved, so close, only a few tables away.

"Meg?" Dawn said hesitantly. "Your eyes are all weird."

I groaned, jerking my attention away from Luke, who'd dropped his beaker and cut his hand in the process.

"Meg?" Dawn sounded scared.

I ignored her. The coppery, intoxicating scent had all of my attention.

"Megan, is there a problem?" My teacher's voice broke through my desire. The long-standing response to authority distracted me from Luke's blood. I stood, half out of my chair, hands white-knuckled around the back of my chair.

"Um. Bathroom. I have to go." I fled while I still had control of myself, barely remembering to grab my books as I dashed into the hallway.

The snow saved me. Shortly after I fled to the girls' bathroom, they announced over the PA that school was closing early. I sighed in relief and hurried to my locker. I remembered Steph only when I saw her hurrying in my direction.

"Not trying to leave me, were you?" She smiled to take any unintended sting out of her words.

"No, sorry. Just been a rough day. I'll tell you about it when we get home. If we're alone." I managed to smile back.

Steph arched her eyebrows and nodded.

I'd figured out two things during the day. I needed to talk to someone, and Steph was the only person I could talk to. A month ago, I could have told Ann, but she was acting too strangely. The other thing I'd figured out was that under no circumstances would I ever go without hunting again. It was too dangerous.

Chapter 8

I threw myself out of the Jeep when we got back to my place, so hungry I had to clench my hands to keep them from shaking, barely noticing the deepening snow as I fled. I could feel Steph's eyes on me, hyper aware of her presence, as I ran inside and upstairs to my bedroom. After a few minutes, she knocked softly on my bedroom door. A pillow over my head did nothing to muffle the smell of her blood.

She called softly from outside my door. "Meg?"

"Just give me a few minutes. I'll be all right." I wasn't sure I'd be okay, but I really didn't have a choice. I had to wait until nightfall to hunt, so I would have to deal.

"Okay. I'm going to make us a snack downstairs. I'll bring it up. If your mom asks, I'll figure something out."

"She's not home."

"Right."

At least she didn't question how I knew. I took several deep breaths and tried to focus on something other than my aching hunger. By the time Steph came back, hesitantly entering the room with two half-full glasses and a plate of cookies, I'd mostly managed.

She grinned sheepishly and held up both glasses. "I thought two glasses would raise fewer questions than one." She sat on my desk chair. Steph glanced over at me after eating a couple of cookies. "So, you gonna tell me what's going on?"

I sighed. "Yeah. Just, um, let me talk, okay?"

"Sure."

Even though I wanted to talk, it took several more minutes before I could speak. "I was too afraid to go hunting last night." I stopped, not wanting to continue. I glanced away from Steph for a minute, shifting uncomfortably on the edge of my bed.

Steph, good to her word, stayed silent, though I could see the questions in her eyes when I looked back at her.

"That girl who was killed. She was my last…" I had no idea what to call her. "I didn't kill her," I rushed on. "Well, I don't know if I did or not. She was alive when I left her. Someplace safe, of course." I buried my face in my hands. "It scared me, but I'm so hungry now, I can barely think. If I was just human, that'd be one thing, but I don't know. I think the hunger will take over, and I won't be able to stop myself if I lose control. It's hard enough when I'm not starving. It's like there is this other thing living inside of me, demanding blood, and I can barely keep it in check. It takes everything I have not to take a little bit more until there's nothing left." I wanted to cry, but I remembered the red tears from last time and managed not to.

Steph shifted her weight, and I wasn't sure if she wanted to comfort me and thought better of touching me, or if she wanted to get further away.

I sighed. "I don't know what to do. If I don't have blood, I'll go crazy, and that wouldn't be good for anyone, but I might have killed that girl."

"You didn't kill her. You said yourself that she was alive when you left her. Someone else must have. We'll have to figure out who." Steph, always the optimist.

"What?" I crossed my arms and glared at Steph.

"We'll have to talk to Gary and his friends. I'm sure they can help."

"Steph, that's dangerous. This person, if it wasn't me, killed someone. We can't go looking for him. He might kill us, too."

"Meg, I hate to remind you of this, but you're damn near indestructible now. And we'll be careful."

I stared at her, not sure what to say.

"It'll be fine."

The familiar rumble of my mom's car in the driveway and the rattle of the garage door saved me from having to come up with an answer.

"Mom's home," I muttered.

I was so grateful when Mom took Steph home. It was probably good practice or something, but I was terrified I would hurt her. I wondered if drug withdrawals felt like this.

Finally dark enough, I wanted to leave the house to hunt even though it was early. Unfortunately, Mom would check on me when she got back. My hands shook while I tried to focus on homework. All I had left was math, usually an easy subject for me. Today, the numbers jumped and blurred on the page as my hunger screamed at me.

Pretending to be asleep made it easy to avoid dinner, and I fell asleep in truth, dark dreams disrupting my rest. The afterimage of glowing, red-rimmed eyes floated in the air in front of me when I woke. A scream caught in my throat and I choked on the breath I'd taken rolling out of bed, certain I was being attacked. Nothing moved in my bedroom, and I slowly rose from my crouch next to my bed. Feeling silly, I was barely able to remember what had sent me into the undignified scramble in the first place.

Once I decided I wasn't in any danger, my hunger tried to take over. I doubled over, clutching my aching stomach. I needed blood. Now. Mom slept down the hall, and while my hunger said perfectly good prey could be found just a door down, I was still conscious enough to be revolted by the thought.

The snow was only a mild hindrance, and I dashed from the house without a coat. Everything but my need was a blur as I hurried toward my normal hunting grounds. Even in my anxious, semi-aware state, I knew going into the bar would be dangerous. The trees and my vampire abilities hid me while I waited. Hot, sweet blood touched my lips, coated my tongue, spilled down my throat. Filled me. I needed more.

I came to my senses as I reached a threshold. I didn't know how I knew, but if I took any more I'd either kill my prey or turn them. Horrified, I flung myself away from the boy I didn't even remember grabbing. He staggered, a blissful expression in his glassy eyes.

"Babe," he slurred. "That was amazing."

I gaped. My food didn't normally talk to me. He staggered a few more steps before leaning up against a tree.

"Damn," he murmured, obviously pleased with himself.

"Come on; you wandered away from the bar. Let's get you safe." My prey repulsed me, now that I could focus on the happy drunk. I still felt hungry, but my hunger was no longer about to take over.

He seemed happy to have my arm around his waist and kept babbling about how wonderful it had been. I was fairly confident he wouldn't remember anything later–a little mind tweaking and a lot of alcohol would see to it–and, at my suggestion, he happily staggered back into the bar, humming.

I ghosted back into the woods, sagging against a damp tree. I could feel the cold, but it didn't bother me as I tried to relax. My wet jeans clung uncomfortably to my legs, and I hoped no one tried to follow my tracks once I decided to trudge back to the road. I needed to get home before anyone noticed I was gone.

It terrified me that I couldn't remember anything before releasing my prey. I hoped no one had seen anything or that I hadn't done anything dumb.

No one saw me as I let myself into my bedroom, though the disturbed snow outside my bedroom window would be an issue if noticed, but I'd deal with it later. I felt tired, and though I was still hungry, I knew I could manage my hunger now. I stripped off my wet clothes, hung my jeans to dry, and fell into bed.

Even vampires needed to sleep.

When my alarm went off in the morning, I hit the snooze and went back to sleep.

It went off again, and I shot my hand out to hit the snooze. I missed, sending my nightstand flying. The alarm gave one more weak buzz and a death rattle before quitting.

I fell asleep again.

"Morning."

"Mmmm?"

"We got more snow last night. School is cancelled, but the sun is out. Let's get some light in here. You're so pale."

I threw myself from the bed as she flung open my curtains, sheets tangling around me, making me feel trapped.

"Megan! Are you okay?"

"Fine," I muttered from the floor between my bed and the wall, trying not to destroy my sheets as I struggled to free myself and keep the panic out of my voice.

"What's wrong, honey? You aren't eating, aren't sleeping right, you're pale as a ghost, and now you're hiding under your bed."

"I'm fine. Just close the curtains."

"Maybe you should see a doctor."

A thrill of terror flooded me with adrenalin–or the vampire equivalent.

"No!" I shouted and took a deep breath. "No, I'm fine." I added a touch of whatever I did to control my victims, hoping it would convince her.

It seemed to work, because she shut the curtains and left. I felt horrible. I didn't know what to do, and after I remade my bed, I crawled back into it, fighting the urge to cry.

Steph and Ann were over by the time I finally made it out of bed later in the afternoon. I could hear them chatting with my mom. She sounded worried, but it seemed like Steph and, to some degree, Ann were doing a pretty good job of reassuring her that, "No, she's not on drugs; we'd know, and no, she's not doing anything she shouldn't. Maybe she has mono or something, but I'm sure she's fine, and I don't think she needs a doctor."

I loved my friends.

I risked a quick glance outside and was relieved to see the sky was back to cloudy gray. It looked like we might get more snow. My skin tingled where the weak light touched it, and I fought the urge to pull away from the window. I wondered what would happen if I stayed in the light. Would I burn away slowly, or would I burst into flames, turn to ash, and float away on the wind?

My skin started to itch, and I stepped away from the window, not really wanting to find out how much of the winter light I could take.

I took a quick shower and dressed, looking forward to a free afternoon.

"Maybe you can use your glamour to make it look like you're actually eating," Steph said a couple of days later as we discussed my mom at lunch.

"My what?"

"You know, your mind-control powers. I think it's called glamour. We'll have to practice."

"Um, okay." I wasn't sure how I felt about my mind-control powers, as they were, but I supposed if they made life easier at home it would have to be okay.

Steph grinned and held out a pencil.

"See if you can make me think there is no pencil in my hand."

I frowned. "Umm. Sure. There is no pencil."

Ann giggled, and Steph gave me an exasperated look.

I stared at the pencil for a moment, wondering how the hell I would do that, when I heard someone sob.

I looked up, glancing at Steph and Ann to see if they had heard. They looked at me, concerned, pencil forgotten.

There'd been another murder.

Chapter 9

Steph and I stared at each other. Her expression mirrored the shock I felt. Ann shifted uncomfortably, smelling of fear and confusion. I hadn't let her in on what I'd told Steph. Normally, I would have, but with her new friends…

As if summoned by my thoughts, the reek of lavender washed over me. I glanced up at the dark-haired girl. I hadn't paid much attention last time she'd come to our table, other than her scent, but now, I studied her more closely. Her hair, dark and Pantene-shiny, fell to her shoulders. She had pale skin; her eyes were blue, and she had a cute button nose with a hint of freckles. Irish descent? I didn't know. She was my height and of average build, leaning toward the athletic side.

I stifled a growl. She was invading my territory, and it really pissed me off.

"Mary Ann." Her voice dripped with sweetness and concern. "Oh, these murders are so terrible. You must be devastated. Why don't you sit with us?"

A soft, angry noise escaped my lips despite my best efforts. She looked at me in surprise as if she just realized I was there. Then she narrowed her eyes and smiled, condescending and pitying at the same time.

"Leave." I growled.

The girl's blue eyes went blank, and she turned without another word and walked away. I stared after her until she left the cafeteria.

Ann managed to look and smell scared and guilty at the same time. Steph seemed more thoughtful, as if she were cataloging the experience.

We were all silent for a moment, as if afraid to speak.

"Sorry," I muttered. "If you want to go hang out with your other friends, I'm not trying to stop you," I said to Ann. "She really ticked me off."

Ann shook her head. "It is okay. She is very self-centered. Candice is much better."

Steph asked, "I've never seen them around before. Have they been here long?"

Ann shrugged. "I do not know. I think they and a couple other people moved here about the same time a month or so ago. I ran into them at the mall, and they seem all right."

Warning bells went off in my head. It seemed like a really odd coincidence. All friends, all moving here at the same time? Or maybe it was because they moved here about the same time as my "accident."

"But they don't want you hanging out with us?" I regretted saying it, but it was too late to take the words back.

Ann's guilty scent spiked, making my nose tingle. I suppressed a sneeze. She muttered something non-committal and stood. "I should check on Candice. She's fragile."

"Well. That was entertaining," I said after Ann walked off.

"Now, if only you could do that all the time." Unflappable, Steph smiled at me.

I wasn't able to actually put a face with the name of the murdered boy until I got home later in the day. Steph came with me, now in the habit of staying over because of the murders. I had a sick feeling in my stomach, and I didn't even have to look at the paper she thrust toward me to know the face would be familiar. I looked anyway, eyes drawn as if to an impending train wreck.

Steph sank heavily into my desk chair.

"When was he killed?" I asked, not wanting to read the article.

"Last night."

"It wasn't me then." I looked again at the smiling face on the front of the page–obviously unaware that, in a few days' time, his charming smile would be extinguished forever.

Steph cocked her head to one side.

"He was…." I still had no idea how to talk about this. I shifted uncomfortably before continuing. "Monday."

"Interesting. They haven't released any details other than that they aren't sure how he died."

"Huh."

Steph nodded. "So, now we need to figure out why this killer is targeting your victims."

She said it casually, as if she wasn't thinking about her words, and the impact they might have. It stung, and I had to fight a quick flash of anger. Victims? I guess the word was accurate, but it hurt to hear it.

"Did I say something wrong?"

A hesitant knock on the front door saved me from having to answer.

"It's Ann," I said.

Surprised, we ran down thc stairs.

"Hi, Ann!"

Ann took a step back at Steph's exuberance, but she smiled, though she faltered for a moment when she looked at me. Then, her grin came back, and she allowed Steph to pull her inside.

"I thought you had plans after school?"

Ann shrugged. "They fell through. No big deal. My parents were not home, and I did not want to be alone."

She told the truth–mostly.

"Meg and I were planning for this weekend."

We were? I shook my head. Steph was pretty excited about her idea, and at this point, I felt obligated to figure out what was going on. My victims were getting killed. I shuddered.

"I don't think any of our parents will let us go out after school with the murders going on." I shrugged. "I mean, maybe if it was summer and still light..."

Steph shook her head. "If we all go together, it should be fine. We're meeting at Steak and Shake. It will be crawling with college students, and we'll promise not to go anywhere with anyone and come straight home when we're done hanging out. It'll be fine," she repeated.

Friday was another cloudy New England day. I made it to school, and though I'm not sure how she did it without mind-control powers, Steph had managed to sweet talk all our parents into letting us go to the diner after classes. College students, high school students, and a few families all gathered around the white tables, eating their steak burgers and slurping their shakes.

I was unbelievably jealous as I watched my friends enjoy their food. Steph and Ann chatted happily about the latest gossip, just like old times. I shrank down in the corner of the booth and tried to be invisible.

It must have worked, because when Gary and two other boys walked up to our table, their gaze slid right over me.

"Hey, Stephanie." Gary grinned that charming smile of his. "Where's Megan?"

I could smell the sharp scent of surprise roll off of Steph, and she looked over to my corner. Ann frowned and glanced at me, too.

"Umm, she'll be right back. Think she had to go to the bathroom." Steph kicked Ann under the table when she opened her mouth to object.

I almost laughed, despite my jealous mood. That would have ruined my spell, or whatever it was, though, so I kept quiet. Unfortunately, now I would to have to wait until the guys left the table before I'd be able to rejoin everyone.

"Let's get a bigger table." Steph stood after a short awkward silence.

Their hesitation gave me a moment to study Gary's friends. One of them was taller, sturdy, and obviously worked out a little. He had short brown hair, brown eyes, and a face that might turn into rugged good looks in fifteen years. His other friend was thin, with slightly longer black hair that probably saw a brush every few days and might have been dyed. His pale skin made it look like he spent more time in front of a computer than he did in the sun.

I gave them all a moment to settle, and then scooted out of the booth and circled around the diner so I could approach from the direction of the bathroom. Once I got out of sight, I concentrated on being here. After a moment, a strange feeling of disassociation I hadn't previously noticed lifted. It freaked me out a little, but I finally forced myself to leave the narrow hallway that led to the bathrooms.

I tried to be inconspicuous as I studied the faces around me. No one pointed at me and exclaimed, "Where did you come from," so I guessed no one had noticed my reappearing act.

Gary saw me first and smiled cautiously. I stiffened, wondering what I had done to earn the wariness in his eyes and the unease that suddenly colored his smell.

Steph twisted around in her seat and rolled her eyes at me. "We moved. I see you found us."

"Megan, these are my friends, Tad"–Gary gestured to the pale thin guy–"and Gage."

I arched my eyebrows at the odd name.

Gage must have been used to the reaction, because he smiled, almost belligerently. "Like a 12 gauge," he said, his voice full of anticipation. "What I'm going to do to the supernatural baddies we find."

I would have laughed, but his eyes were serious, and it drove home–one more time–that I was one of the "supernatural baddies" now. I wondered how he'd feel about me if he knew. I forced a smile, though it felt more like my lips twisted into an ugly grimace to match the sour feeling in my stomach.

It seemed to be enough for Gage. He leaned back into his chair as if satisfied with my reaction. "So what do we know?" Gary said.

"Well, we know we have something weird going on." Steph put her elbows on the table and rested her chin on her hands.

Gary nodded. "Yeah, a serial killer. Weird. They won't release details of death either. They just keep saying that it is unknown."

"Tad found out that all the bodies were low on blood. Not like they'd been drained by a vampire or anything, but as if they'd suffered blood loss a few days before. Other than that, there wasn't a mark on them."

I tried not to squirm, especially when Steph glanced at me. I shrugged. What did she want me to say? That the blood loss was my fault and had little to do with the cause of death? Yeah, right.

"Do they have any theories?"

Tad shook his head.

I asked, "Could it have been a heart attack?"

"Coroner said no," Tad said.

"Well, then that's our first mission. To find out who is killing these people." Steph grinned.

"Umm, I hate to break it to you, but chasing down a serial killer is really not a good idea." I felt I had to point that out.

Steph gave me a look I interpreted as, *But we have you.*

"Besides, there is no sign that these are supernatural killings," I protested weakly. I am not a hero. This was a bad idea.

"If we're going to fight supernatural crime, we have to start somewhere," Gary said.

Obviously, they weren't going to listen to reason, so I slumped into my chair and fell silent. Gary started to say something else, but before he could get very far, a shadow darkened our table. Surprised I hadn't sensed anyone coming, my alarm bells went off at the sight of the tall, dark-haired, handsome guy who walked up to our table. He couldn't have been much older than us, but something felt really odd about him.

"Mary Ann," he purred. "I'm happy to see you here. Would you like to join me?"

I gaped at her reaction to him, a combination of lust and anticipation. I fought the urge to growl at the newcomer. Something told me I wouldn't win as easily against him as I had the girl who reeked of lavender.

"Hi, Alexander." Ann smiled a stupid little grin she couldn't have been aware of. She stood without even looking at us.

Alexander held out one arm, and Ann slid her arm through it. Her worshipful gaze never left his face, even when he looked back over his shoulder and met my eyes.

A shock sparked its way through my body, electrifying nerve endings and making the little hairs on the back of my neck stand on end, but it was nothing compared to the way his intense blue gaze held mine. Power spiked through me as if trying to invade my core, capture me, and make me his. Briefly immobilized, anger slammed through me, shoving at the power trying to pierce me. It receded quickly, and Alexander arched an eyebrow and gave me a cocky leer. Just testing, that arrogant grin said.

I glared after him as he sauntered away with my friend on his arm. A soft growl escaped my lips, but something beyond sheer territoriality set me on edge. I was afraid of Alexander, deeply afraid, and that made me even angrier.

Chapter 10

"Meg," Steph whispered. "Shut your eyes."

It took me a moment to realize what she really meant. I shut them and took deep breaths, trying to calm myself and turn my eyes back to their normal shade of brown.

By the time I had myself under control, Gary, Tad, and Gage were also looking at me.

Gage asked, "You okay, dude?"

I muttered that I was fine.

"Who was that?" Tad stared after them.

Steph shook her head, forehead creased in confusion. "I've never seen him before."

"Mary Ann obviously knows him," I finally said, voice still deepened with a growl.

"Megan, what's wrong?"

"He feels so wrong."

"Sure you're not jealous?" Steph frowned. Anyone else I might have hit just then.

"Jealous of what?" I snarled. "That she might have a boyfriend? I don't care about that. I'd be happy about that, but he's wrong somehow."

Steph recoiled. I forced myself back into my seat and took more deep breaths.

"Sorry."

"It's okay."

"I thought she was your best friend," Tad finally said.

"She is." Steph seemed confused.

"Apparently some new people moved in a few months back." I managed to make my tone sound normal. "We've seen them around school, but until the other day, I'd never seen Ann with them. She's been acting a bit odd recently, and I'm not sure why she hasn't mentioned them before. We've been best friends for a very long time. I suppose she might have been worried we'd be mad about her hanging out with other people, but even Steph and I have other friends. It's not a huge deal, but it seems like they are trying to steal her away."

"Huh," Gage said. "Weird."

Gary put his hands on the table and stared at them for a few moments before speaking. "All right. We'll see what we can find out. Tad has been monitoring the internet for odd happenings, but hasn't really seen anything yet. Perhaps now that we have some sort of focus it will help."

Tad nodded. "I'll start compiling information for our next meeting."

"Start a couple of months back." I tried not to meet Tad's eyes. I didn't want him to ask why.

Tad arched an eyebrow at me, and I practically expected him to tell me to live long and prosper.

Gary cut in. "Good idea. We can see if there are any odd occurrences building up to this. Also, we'll look into the newbies." He gestured toward Ann.

I followed his hand and had to suppress another flash of jealousy as Alexander took a long drink out of his shake. Whatever he was, it didn't keep him from eating.

"We'll do what we can as well," Steph said.

Gary asked, "Good. Any chance you guys will be able to get over here on Sunday?"

"Maybe." I really didn't want to commit to anything, but Steph apparently felt more confident.

"Yeah, it shouldn't be an issue."

"Great!" Gary smiled at Steph, and I couldn't help but notice her blush when she smiled back.

I fought another flash of jealousy.

Steph pulled out her cell phone and glanced at the display. "We should probably get going, or your mom is going to start calling us."

"We need to, um, rescue Ann before we can get out of here." Steph started texting. "I'll see if I can get her attention."

We waited for Ann to check her phone. She always had it on. But after five minutes and one more text, we admitted defeat.

"Okay, Plan Two. Meg, take out Alexander. Gage and I can grab Ann. Tad and Gary can start a food fight as a diversion."

I stared at her, trying to figure out if she was actually serious.

"Why does she get to take on Alexander?" Gage grumbled.

"Because she knows martial arts," Steph said matter-of-factly.

I sighed in relief. Steph was joking, though I could tell the guys weren't quite sure. "Okay, on to the real Plan Two, because I'm pretty sure my rusty martial arts skills are no match for Alexander." I shuddered, remembering how his eyes had grabbed me, tried to caress my soul, and steal my mind.

"You're no fun."

I laughed. Probably the first real laugh I'd had in quite some time. "I think we're going to have to suck it up and go get her." I was not looking forward to that.

"Let's pay, then we'll go with you." Gary stood.

"Okay." Hopefully, safety in numbers would help.

I could feel Alexander's eyes on us as we went up to the counter, though the one time I actually looked, he was focused on Ann. Once we paid, we headed over to Ann's table, with me at the head of the pack. I don't know how I got elected leader, but I guess that was fine; I could take more damage.

Alexander raised his shocking blue eyes when we approached. He had the gall to look surprised, and surveyed our numbers before smiling slightly.

"Yes?"

"We came to get Ann." My voice remained surprisingly steady. "We have to leave, and we can't go without her."

"Oh?"

Ann still stared raptly at Alexander. It seemed too much like some sort of mind control for my liking.

"Yeah. Our parents said we could come out, but only if we stayed together."

"She'll be safe with me," he purred.

I doubted that. Hell, she might not be entirely safe with me if it came down to it. "I'm sure you think so, but she still has to come with us. Parents' rules. Surely you can understand."

Alexander didn't appear to be much older than any of us, maybe a college student, yet his eyes held age and wisdom that freaked me out. He wasn't a vampire–I was pretty sure–but whatever he was, it wasn't completely human. I also got the impression he knew exactly what I was.

He smiled slowly, as if he could sense my train of thought. Yes, his nod said. I know what you are, little girl, and it doesn't scare me.

I tried not to shudder. I didn't want him to know he was getting to me.

"Very well. Mary Ann, your friends want you to go with them." She seemed to ignore his words.

It took me a moment, but after a brief inner struggle, I could focus again, anger threatening to overwhelm me. "Ann." I added a touch of something to my voice to get her attention.

She blinked, and Alexander gave me a brief, condescending smile as if to say, good job.

Ann turned her head slowly as if waking from a deep sleep. "Hi, Meg." She almost sounded normal.

"Come on, Ann, we need to get going."

"I'm fine with Alexander."

"I know, Ann, but Mom said we could only come if we stayed together. That means you have to go home with us, or she won't let us out of the house without her again. If you want to meet up with Alexander later, that's fine." It wasn't fine, but whatever.

Ann sighed. "All right. I'll see you later."

He nodded, blue eyes glinting with amusement.

Ann pushed back her chair and stood. She moved normally, but it still seemed like she wasn't all there. I didn't like that it seemed as if Alexander had messed with Ann's head, and regardless of whatever else was going on, I would find a way to stop him from doing it. Steph and I traded worried glances, but she followed us willingly enough out of the Steak and Shake.

I led the way to my Jeep and was sticking my key in the lock when I realized the guys were still following us. Some super alert hunter of the night I was.

"So, Sunday?" Gary asked once he had our attention again.

I nodded. "We'll do our best."

"Give me your number in case we can't get away," Steph said to Gary.

Apparently, she wasn't as confident about Sunday as she'd seemed. Or maybe she just wanted his phone number. Gary nodded and fished in his pocket for a scrap of paper. I handed him a pen from my Jeep, and he scribbled for a moment.

"I put my email address there, too. Feel free to contact me. It might help if we can get in touch over email. That way if we find something out between meetings, we can share."

It was a great idea, and it was pretty cool that he didn't demand our information in return, giving us the choice. It made me trust him a little bit more.

Steph pocketed the note and smiled. "Sure. I'll do that when I get home.

"Thanks."

I watched as they walked across the parking lot and climbed into an old pickup. Gage was driving. Somehow, that didn't surprise me at all.

We hurried into the Jeep. Hyper-aware of the darkness that surrounded us, I felt it sing in my bones, begging me to go run through the night, to take it in, and become one with it. I had a hard time resisting, but I needed to get Steph and Ann back to my place. There was a killer on the loose, and I was at least partially responsible for his choice in victims. I felt bad enough about that, but I was terrified he'd start targeting my friends.

We stopped at my place briefly to reassure my mom that we were alive. She wanted us to talk to her in person, and it wasn't too far out of the way to Steph's house where we were spending the night.

We ran inside, and I grabbed my bags, briefly stopping to hug Mom. She looked and smelled so worried that I didn't protest when she made me promise to call from the landline when we reached Steph's house. Personally, I thought she was overreacting, but at least she let me leave the house, so I didn't complain.

The uncomfortable silence during the drive through the dark, vacant streets made the trip seem much longer than the normal ten minutes. We'd all grown up in the same neighborhood, which is one of the reasons we were best friends. However, both Ann's and Steph's parents had moved during our fifth grade year, and now, we had to travel a little to see each other. It wasn't a big deal now that we could drive, though only I actually had a car. Mine was a hand-me-down from my brother. After making me swear a solemn promise to take care of it while he was deployed, he'd handed me the keys. I'd tried to hide my excitement, tainted as it was with his leaving, but still, I had a car, and I did take good care of it.

When I pulled into the driveway and killed the engine, the silence was deafening. I opened my door and stepped out into the crisp air. There were still several inches of snow on the ground, and it had the old, used, and slightly dirty quality I'd never liked.

"Meg," Steph said.

"Hmm?" I jerked my attention away from the snow-covered ground.

"You might want to consider wearing a coat."

I looked at her, confused, before looking at my arms. I'd apparently forgotten mine at home. My pale skin showed no evidence of being cold, no goose bumps, no bluish tinge.

"Thanks." I shivered reflexively, though I wasn't cold.

"Let's go inside."

"Sure." I grabbed my bags and helped Ann with hers before following Steph into the house. Once we were settled in the basement, had pizza ordered, and a movie playing in the background, Steph turned on her laptop and stared at the screen. "So, Ann. Who's your friend?"

Ann blushed. I could smell the heat of her blood come close to the surface, and it reminded me of my growing hunger. I shifted uncomfortably.

"Um. A friend."

"We gathered as much." Steph's voice was dry.

"Ann, it's cool if you have a boyfriend. That's fine. He's just creepy, like he's trying to steal you away, and well...he's really creepy."

Ann burst into tears. Steph and I traded a shocked look.

"I knew you would say that," she sobbed. "That is why I did not tell you, but he is really, really nice, and he likes me and..." She sniffed.

"Ann, it's okay. Really. Meg's creepy, too. We're good with that. We're your friends, and we want to make sure that everything is okay."

I glared at Steph, but right now it wasn't worth the argument. Creepy? Me? No. Never.

"Everything is fine." She sobbed.

Steph and I exchanged another look.

Chapter 11

We avoided the topic of Alexander for the rest of the night. Instead, we focused on researching the victims on the internet. There seemed to be little in common between them, but we weren't trained investigators. Of course, we were familiar with the one factor linking them–me.

I still avoided thinking about it. When it finally got late enough, and I got so hungry that I couldn't ignore my needs anymore, I cast a guilty look at my friends before muttering that I needed to go out. Steph and Ann managed not to look disgusted, but I could sense their unease. I slunk through the quiet house and out into the bright, snow-filled night.

They let me sleep late into the afternoon the next day, and by the time I got home, it was well into the evening, which was fine with me. For once, I didn't have much homework, and it only took me about half an hour to finish it. I spent the rest of my time pretending to do schoolwork and avoiding Mom.

Steph had given me some reading assignments, one of them being Dracula. I alternately felt sick inside and highly amused as I read the dark tale, glad I didn't have to tote around large coffins full of dirt.

After a while, even my morbid fascination with the book couldn't distract me from my growing hunger, and may have added to it. So I put the book down and contemplated the murders. Because the murderer targeted my victims, I could conclude I'd been observed, at least those times. So I needed to be more careful. I felt like kicking myself. How else would it know who to kill?

It hunted at night as well. Could it go out during the day? I could, sort of. So far, it had only targeted two of my victims, so maybe it had only seen me twice. Maybe it didn't need to feed very often. I rolled these ideas around in my head, getting frustrated. I didn't even know why it would go after those I'd fed from. Was it because they were weaker and easier prey? Was it to target me?

Steph worked her magic yet again, and Sunday afternoon found us back at the Steak and Shake. I wanted a burger so badly–with mayo and onions and a touch of mustard for some tang. I sat in stony silence while Steph and Gary chatted happily, and tried to ignore the savory smell of the meat and the creamy sweetness of the shakes. The mouth-watering scent almost made me try and eat, though I knew from past experience that it would go badly.

Ann would meet us there, and though she hadn't said, Steph and I had guessed she was with Alexander again. I kept telling myself it was fine, but he really freaked me out. I felt awkward around Gary, Tad, and Gage, and I was generally cranky.

"Meg?"

I ground my teeth.

"Meg?"

"What!" I finally recognized that someone was actually talking to me, not just about me. Steph flinched, and I apologized.

"You gonna make it?"

I gave her a you-have-got-to-be-kidding-me look. I had already told her we needed a new place to meet. I don't think she had quite understood.

"Dude. Just eat a burger and relax," Gage said.

I shoved back from the table. "Just let me know when you've figured out more ways to get us killed," I growled and stalked out the front door, leaving a stunned silence in my wake.

Outside was a little sunnier than I would have liked, despite the blanket of grayish clouds, but I would make it. The meager light, reflected from the white-covered ground, made it distinctly uncomfortable. I found a spot under a bare tree that was marginally less sunny and leaned against the rough trunk. After a moment, I realized I wasn't wearing a jacket, but I decided I didn't care.

The diner sat on the edge of the only shopping center in the area, and I watched the bustle of people as they moved between the buildings and the cars. I wasn't sure if it was my own paranoia coloring my senses, but it seemed like people looked over their shoulders more often than they used to.

A familiar scent caught my attention, and I turned in time to see Ann getting out of a small white sedan. The hairs on the back of my neck rose, and a chill ran down my spine as Alexander got out of the front seat and gave her a hug. I was surprised when they didn't kiss, but Ann smiled as she stepped away and gave a quick wave before walking toward the diner. She scanned the parking lot until her gaze settled on my Jeep before entering the restaurant.

Relatively convinced she was safe for the time being, I shifted my attention back to Alexander. He watched Ann, a small smile on his face. Then he frowned and glanced in my direction. I ducked behind the tree, hoping it would hide me. I could feel his attention directed toward me, but after a moment, it faded, and I risked looking.

Alexander got into his car. I waited while he pulled away, then without really thinking, I took off after him. I could dodge through the thick forest of hardwoods and remain unseen while I raced after his car. I concentrated on being not here while I ran, aware that Alexander might have other senses than just his eyes.

I followed him for several miles to a ritzy neighborhood hidden away amongst the trees, most of the houses isolated from each other by space and forest. I slipped through the woods, following Alexander through several more turns to a three-story house with a wraparound porch. It was tucked back away from the street and surrounded by bare-branched hardwoods. He pulled into the driveway and parked to the side of the two-car garage. I hid and observed as he climbed out of his car, stopped, and looked around. He frowned, and I wondered if he knew he was being followed.

He stopped scanning the forest and moved closer to the house, and I followed him. This time of year there was no way I would find an open window, but I might be able to hear enough through one to find out more about him.

I slunk around, glancing in windows, catching glimpses of nice furnishings, spare decorations, and a lit fireplace. I ducked when I saw Alexander walk into the kitchen, and stretched out my senses to see if I could detect anyone else in the house.

It seemed like Alexander lived alone. I had almost expected Ann's other friends to live with him as well, if they were actually connected to any of the strange things going on.

A loud ring made me jump, and I thought I heard Alexander swear quietly before he picked up the receiver.

"Hello?" His voice had lost most of the arrogant smoothness, and he sounded scared when he spoke again. "No, I wasn't followed. I'm sure. No, I haven't found anything. She doesn't know anything. She doesn't even know what she is."

I felt a cold thrill ripple through my body. Was he talking about me? Why would he be? I supposed he could be talking about Ann, but I didn't think so.

"No. I haven't found it. I'll keep looking." Alexander sighed. "I am trying to hurry. I know time is of the essence." He paused again. "Bye."

I jumped and rubbed my ears when Alexander slammed the phone down on the receiver. Hearing still enhanced, I could hear Alexander's footsteps coming closer. I flattened myself against the house, sure he was going to look out the window. Somehow, he had sensed me.

"Maybe I was followed," he muttered.

Trying to hide, I pressed myself more firmly to the ground, trying to make myself as invisible as possible. I gasped as something seemed to grab me by my shoulders and hips. Before I could do more than flail a little, it yanked me down through the snow. The ground embraced me into its cold, safe, comforting depths, and before I could really think about panicking, it lulled me to sleep.

Chapter 12

Night had fallen when the ground released me from its embrace. Slowly, I opened my eyes, feeling more rested than I had in ages. I looked around, expecting to find myself in my bed. Instead, I lay in the snow, curled up against someone's house. I sat up quickly and tried to get my bearings.

It took me a moment to remember where I was, and once I did, I panicked, certain I'd been discovered. I hastily reached out with my senses and calmed myself. No one was around.

I got up slowly, brushing away the clinging snow and dashed into the forest. I had to get back to my friends.

Cars crowded the parking lot, and my Jeep sat where I'd left it. So I probably wasn't gone long enough for them to report me as missing. But I still had no idea how long I'd been away or what the hell had happened.

I concentrated on the Steak and Shake for a moment and was relieved to sense Steph and Ann inside. I thought the guys might still be with them, and I couldn't sense Alexander's peculiar feel at all, which made me excessively happy. One last time I took a moment to make sure I wasn't covered in dirt. I felt like I should be.

The diner was crowded when I entered, and I was hyper aware of the press of high school and college students around me, their blood pulsing below the surface of their skin, their–I jerked myself out of my train of thought. It was bad enough that I had to feed on them. I didn't have to think about it all the time.

"Meg!" Steph's voice filled with concern.

Ann shot me a concerned glance, and even the guys seemed worried.

Steph asked, "Where were you?"

"Walking. Sorry." Obviously, I couldn't tell them here, and I wasn't sure I wanted to tell Ann at all since it was her boyfriend I had followed.

Steph and Ann let it go, but the guys still had questions in their eyes. I tried not to appear guilty when I looked at them. I wasn't sure how well I succeeded, but they didn't say anything.

"We should get going," Steph said into the awkward silence. "Our parents were expecting us just after dark."

"Sure." Gary stared at me.

I shifted uncomfortably before stepping away from the table.

"Meg."

I turned and left before Gary could say anything else. I heard Steph apologize for me, and irrationally, it made me even angrier. She said something about stress, which I supposed could be true.

I waited for Ann and Steph by my car and managed to cool down by the time they arrived, thankfully without the guys in tow. Neither said anything while I pulled out of the parking lot. The trip to Ann's house was full of tense silence. I wanted to break it, but I really had no idea what to say.

"So, what the hell happened?" Steph turned to me as soon as Ann was inside her house and I had pulled out of the driveway.

"I followed Alexander after he dropped Ann off. I overheard a phone conversation I don't quite understand. He's not a normal human, though, whatever he is. He's looking for something, and he says time is short. I couldn't hear what the other person said. Then I think he noticed me outside. I tried to hide and somehow the ground swallowed me. Maybe it was some sort of spell around his house, but whatever happened, it didn't let me go until the sun set. I slept really well."

"I'm not quite sure what to say about that. What possessed you to follow Alexander?"

I shrugged. "He creeps me out, and it seemed like the thing to do. I know where he lives now, but we still don't know anything about Candice and the other girl. Nothing about them made me think they weren't human, but still...."

"Meg, we were worried sick."

"Of the six of us, I think I'm probably the one you have to worry about least."

Steph shut her eyes for a minute. "Maybe. I have to fill you in on what Tad found. You may not feel so confident then."

"Um."

"We don't have time now. I'll tell you tomorrow at school. Just be careful tonight, okay?"

I clenched my jaw at the reminder of what I had to do tonight, but gave Steph a curt nod.

Mom was waiting when I arrived home, but she didn't say anything other than "Hi." She smelled worried rather than angry, and I wondered if Steph would be able to sweet-talk her into letting us go out again.

At least going to Steak and Shake gave me an excuse to avoid dinner. Mom looked stressed, but I was afraid to start a conversation, because I didn't want her to start asking awkward questions. So, I dashed up to my room. I did have homework to do, and it gave me a good excuse to remain antisocial. It also kept me occupied until it got late enough to sneak out.

Crisp and vibrant, the air made me feel alive as the night caressed my skin. The currents pulsed through me. I shivered, joy singing through my veins, and started to run. I had no real destination in mind. I just wanted to be one with the night.

I made it home right before dawn, feeling better than I had in months. I'd fed, but that seemed secondary to the overall contentment. I wondered if it had anything to do with getting sucked into the ground. Several of the books Steph had given me seemed to indicate some vampires slept in dirt. I wasn't sure how I felt about it, but I couldn't deny that I felt well-rested.

My room seemed undisturbed when I crawled through my window. Relieved, I quickly changed clothes and fell into bed for a few hours of sleep before school.

"Did you see anything last night?" Steph asked me at lunch.

I looked up from my textbook and frowned, the image of the deer I'd stalked for several hours coming to mind, how her winter-puffed fur had moved gently in the wind, each hair vibrant, standing out from the other. How her breath had misted from her nose and her dewy eyes had darted about as if she'd known something watched her. How her energies flowed out from her, melding with the night and giving her a sense that humans didn't even suspect deer had.

Somehow, I didn't think that's what she wanted to know about. She must have sensed my confusion.

"Was there anyone following you?"

"Oh. No, I don't think so."

"You don't think so? Meg..." Steph frowned.

I shrugged. "Trust me. I paid attention. Nothing I could sense was following me."

"Okay."

Steph fell silent, and I had a feeling she wanted to say more. I was about to ask her what Tad had found when Ann joined us.

"Did you tell her what Tad found?" Ann asked her, echoing my thoughts.

Steph shook her head. "Not yet.

"So what did Tad find that has you so freaked out?" I tried to keep my tone light.

"Well, Tad says he thinks he found a forum where at least some of the members might actually be real, um, supernatural critters."

"Do you know how many crazy people are out there pretending to be vampires or witches or whatever?"

Steph looked at me for a moment before responding, her voice quiet. "You do realize there are at least two real vampires."

"Fine. So there are a bunch of wackos on a message board that might also contain supernatural wackos. So what?" I really had a hard time containing my increasingly grumpy mood–the good feelings from last night and this morning, gone. The brief reminder that someone out there had attacked and abandoned me didn't help.

Steph took a deep breath, so I opened my eyes. The expression on her face looked strained, as if she were fighting anger. I cautiously reached out with my senses, trying to get a feel for her mood, and was surprised to catch the sour, intoxicating smell of real fear under her annoyance.

"Steph, what's wrong? You're afraid." I almost added, "Is it me?" but didn't, not wanting the answer.

"How do you know?"

I opened my mouth, and then snapped it shut. I'd forgotten I hadn't shared that tidbit with them. I really hated all this. "I can smell fear, and well...I guess, emotion," I finished in a quiet rush.

"Oh."

Ann asked, "All the time?"

"Well, at first, yeah, but I figured out how to turn it off, mostly." Then it dawned on me I'd basically admitted I was purposefully trying to sense Steph's emotions. Oh, well. Add it to my creepiness.

Steph and Ann seemed to mull this around for a moment before Steph shrugged. "That could be handy."

I nodded, not quite meeting her eyes. "Yeah, sure. Anyway, you were saying? Wackos?"

Steph smiled, and I actually made Ann giggle.

"Right. So. This forum Tad found seems, at least to him, to have some legitimacy hidden amongst the wackos. And what he is hearing is disturbing. There is something out there hunting vampires."

"Um, like human hunters or what?"

"He doesn't know, but he says he's been monitoring it for a couple of months, and every once in a while, a regular poster will comment that someone is following them. Then they aren't heard from again. Of course, Tad and Gage were not terribly concerned about something knocking off vampires, but we were." She gestured to Ann, who nodded.

"Okay. But they could be anywhere, right? Doesn't mean it's here."

Steph nodded. "Right, and most of them aren't, but the last several posters who disappeared were near here. Obviously, they could be lying about their locations, but Tad could correlate a higher instance of unexplained murders with their disappearances. He thinks it's significant–and he is a math minor."

"That doesn't surprise me somehow."

Steph grinned. "You'd like him if you gave him a chance."

"Why, because we're both good at math?" I rolled my eyes, and then couldn't resist adding, "And we're both creepy?"

Steph laughed. "Something like that."

"We just want you to be careful. You could be a target."

I held up my hand to cut her off and jerked my head toward an approaching lavender-scented cloud. Ann glanced over her shoulder and nodded.

"Mary Ann." Ann's friend leaned over our table. I wondered what her name was. Though I could identify her by her reek, I didn't think either Steph or Ann would appreciate me calling her "reeks of lavender" out loud.

"Hi, Jennifer," Ann said softly.

"Are you going to join us?" She sniffed.

"Later."

Jennifer actually seemed surprised, though I couldn't smell anything over the lavender stench. "Okay." She turned, not bothering to acknowledge me or Steph and sauntered away.

"Nice girl. I like her," I muttered.

Ann nodded. "She is a bit overbearing."

"Understatement," Steph said matter-of-factly.

Ann giggled again.

I smiled. Things were starting to feel much more normal. Though I wasn't very concerned about someone hunting me, I was curious about this forum of Tad's. Maybe I could get some answers.

Chapter 13

Maybe because of Steph and Ann's concern, or maybe because I was becoming a better vampire–whatever the hell that meant–I started to be more careful at night, more observant. There were a couple of times I thought I had been followed, though I managed to lose whatever shadowed me before I fed.

The next two murders were people I'd never heard of from the college. We also managed two more meetings with the guys. They had found some interesting correlations, further convincing Steph that whatever it was hunted vampires. I wasn't convinced, but then, I still really wasn't convinced vampires actually existed, even though I was one. I kept expecting to wake up and discover this had all been some horrible nightmare, and everything had gone back to normal.

Gary hadn't tried to talk to me outside of our group conversations since the day I'd followed Alexander. Though I did catch him looking at me now and again with a thoughtful expression on his face, and I'd heard him ask Steph once what was wrong with me. She'd said, "Nothing," but she'd said it too quickly. I doubted Gary believed her.

Overall, despite the murders, things did begin to settle down. Ann acted more normal now that we'd, at least marginally, accepted Alexander. They were getting used to me. I was getting used to me. Also, true to winter in the New England states, the sun remained hidden behind clouds, and I didn't have to play sick to skip school.

I let these thoughts distract me as I stalked through the night toward The Long Branch, the bar I liked. The temperature had dropped enough that lurking on campus and finding wayward students would have been difficult during normal times. Now with the murders, everyone traveled in pairs. Perhaps if I had more practice using my powers, I'd be able to deal with it, but I couldn't yet.

I slipped into the warm, crowded bar, and concentrated on not being noticed. I was getting pretty good at that trick, and I found my way to a corner booth.

Unfortunately, even here people were pairing up more than usual. So I followed the first single person I saw, a curvy blonde woman, who staggered more than once as she left the smoky bar.

I slipped out after her and sighed when she headed to a car. For one, she shouldn't be driving, and two, that might make it harder for me. I hurried to catch up, the chilly air invigorating, the rush of the hunt filling me. I made myself slow down as I neared the woman, and forced myself into a calm facade.

"Hey, you shouldn't be driving," I said when I got close enough.

"Too far to walk," she slurred, sounding resigned and depressed. I wasn't sure if the alcohol had depressed her or something else, but it didn't really matter.

"I'll drive you." I added power to my voice to convince her. "It'll be fine. Where do you live?"

Her eyes, if possible, went even glassier. She held out her keys, moving woodenly as if being controlled by something else.

"Campus Sorority Row."

Now, I really wondered why she drank alone. I took her keys and helped her into the passenger side of the car before sliding into the driver's side and turning the key in the ignition. The car rumbled to life, and I backed the unfamiliar, boat-like sedan out of the parking spot and headed toward campus.

The girl quickly fell unconscious, and it was easy for me to pull over and feed. It was getting easier to drink from girls. Necessity being a bitch and all.

When I finished, I drove the rest of the way to the college. I didn't know exactly where the sorority houses were, but I had a good guess, and it didn't take me long to find them. I found a free parking spot and helped the groggy woman out of her car, again wondering why she had come out alone. Her blood tasted of corruption, as if she were sick. It didn't bother me, beyond the odd sensation. I'd tasted it before to some degree from a few of my other victims, but so far, it seemed strongest in her.

I leaned her against the entryway to the house she indicated and rang the doorbell before slipping into the shadows and watching to make sure someone helped her inside.

Before too long, I heard footsteps, and the door opened a crack.

"Chelsea!" the girl who answered the door said loudly. "What's wrong?"

Chelsea mumbled something about drinking too much and stumbled inside with her sorority sister's help. After hearing the distinctive snick of a deadbolt shutting, I crept away from the big house and, not having much better to do, decided to wander around campus. I wasn't sure if I wanted to walk openly or hide in the shadows, so I decided to do both, hiding as best I could across the large open commons and walking openly amongst the buildings.

There were people out, even as late as it was on this cool, crisp night, walking in pairs, laughing about the cold, boys, or stressing about upcoming exams. I fought growing jealousy at the normalcy of their lives.

About to leave, a shrill, inhuman cry split the night and sent me to my knees. It seemed to vibrate in my bones, sending shards of metaphorical glass through my core, shredding my body as if it was tissue paper. I clutched my ears, trying to drown it out, certain if it kept going, my mind would shatter like crystal.

Just as suddenly as the cry started, it stopped. I opened my eyes, looking at my hands, surprised they weren't covered in blood, flesh ripped from bone. I flexed my intact fingers and shuddered before climbing slowly to my feet. I wasn't sure when I'd fallen completely to the ground, nor was I sure how long the banshee wail had lasted, but the sky looked noticeably lighter in the east. I shivered again and turned toward home.

My ears were still ringing, or at least that's the excuse I gave myself when I realized someone human was screaming and probably had been for a while. I debated ignoring the scream and going home, but I was running before I'd made the conscious decision to find out what had happened.

By the time I arrived, a crowd had gathered at the front steps of the sorority house. My stomach sank, and my knees went weak. The crowd parted around me at my unconscious use of power, and I found myself staring at a familiar blonde-haired girl, throat torn out, blood coating the front of her shirt, but oddly enough, not leaking to the ground. I hadn't taken so much blood that pools of it shouldn't be soaking into the ground beneath her, so whatever had killed her had taken the rest.

Shuddering, I looked up at the crowd, sensing familiar presences. I was surprised to see Gary, Tad, and Gage. I looked away, sensing someone else, and met Alexander's shocking blue gaze. We stared at each other for a minute, something akin to hate in his eyes. I wasn't sure what he saw in mine, but I glanced back at the body before looking at him again. Only…Alexander had left.

Gary said my name, but I ignored him, melting backward out of the crowd, searching for Alexander. Sirens blared in the distance, and I knew I had to get out of there, or I'd never get inside before the sun rose. It looked like it might be one of those rare, bright days, and I had no desire to find out what would happen if I got caught out in it.

"Meg!"

I stopped, not able to ignore him any longer without attracting attention. Gary stopped close to me, Gage and Tad scanning the surrounding area. All three of them were panting as if they had been running, breath fogging in the cool air.

"Did you see anything?"

"What?"

"Did you see anything, before she was killed?"

"No. Just the horrible wail." I shivered.

Gary frowned. "What?"

"The wailing beforehand. I thought my head was going to explode."

Gary traded a look with Tad and Gage, who both shook their heads no.

"We didn't hear anything."

I glanced east again. I had to get home. "Look. I need to get going. We can talk about this later."

"Meg, you're a witness."

"Yeah, the police are going to buy that. 'Oh, officer, it was terrible. There was this inhuman screeching that seemed like it was going to tear the skin from my bones, then someone human started screaming.'" I gave my worst helpless-girl imitation.

Gary gave me an even look.

"Besides, I'm not exactly supposed to be out, and if I don't get back, Mom will notice I'm missing. I have to go."

"Fine, but we need to talk about this later."

"Right."

Tad asked, "What were you doing out, anyway?"

I snorted and decided to give them the truth, though they'd take it differently. I hoped. "I was hunting. What are you doing out?"

Tad smiled. "Hunting."

"Damn straight." Gage growled.

I rolled my eyes. "I have to go." Before they could delay me any longer, I took off running at a normal human pace, until I went around the corner of a building. Then, I sprinted as fast as I could. I had to get home before the sun came up.

The house was quiet when I got home, but even before I climbed back into my empty bedroom, I knew something wasn't right. The feeling was confirmed when I saw the crack of light filtering around the door I knew I'd left shut.

"Shit."

Chapter 14

I forced myself out of bed, obscenely early for a Saturday, dressed and slunk down the stairs, hoping to avoid notice as long as possible.

"Megan!" Mom yelled with a surprising lack of tension in her voice.

I jumped, my system coursing with the instinct to run. I took a couple of deep breaths to calm myself before going into the living room. I stopped outside, sensing someone else, the presence oddly familiar. I walked the last few steps into the living room, trying to figure out who the other person was, and stared, shocked when I saw my brother John. He smiled at me and stood. I threw myself into his arms, careful not to overbalance him with my vampire strength.

"Hey, kiddo." He laughed.

"Hi! You're home!" I was so happy I had to force myself not to smile too much to avoid showing off my fangs. We did not need to have that discussion.

"It was a surprise. I got in last night."

I felt a cold thrill run through me. Maybe it had been John, and not Mom, who had found me missing. That might be better. Then again, it might not.

"How long will you be here?"

"A couple of weeks." John took a step back and studied me. I met his happy gaze, studying him back. His very short hair framed the same brown eyes, but he looked leaner and tanner. I also studied him with my new senses. He was tired. Stress made his otherwise pleasant sense slightly sour. But I sensed no fear, which reassured me.

I was about to hammer him with questions when I caught the familiar sensation that was Steph, heading toward the front door. Once I knew she was there, I could hear the quiet rumble of her mom's car.

"Huh." I turned toward the door.

"What?"

"Steph's here," I said quietly, a little confused as I went to answer the door moments before she knocked.

"You see what I was talking about?" I heard Mom whisper to John. "She's acting strange."

"I'd hardly call knowing when her best friend is going to be at the door completely crazy. I heard the car, too, just didn't recognize it." He covered for me.

I opened the door, not quite able to hide my grin.

Steph turned and waved at her mom before frowning. "What's up?"

I grabbed her hand–to her credit, she didn't flinch–and dragged her into the living room.

"John!" She positively squealed. I'd never heard Steph squeal before. I laughed as she threw herself into my brother's arms.

Cute and nice and only a couple of years older than us, Ann and Steph had secretly harbored crushes on John for years. Late night slumber party confessions had revealed that secret, but it had never bothered me.

"Hi, Steph." John laughed.

"Hi, Steph," Mom repeated.

"Hi, Mrs. Taylor. I'm sorry to intrude, but I was going to see if Meg wanted to hang out."

"Oh, you're not intruding."

"Of course not," John added. "You're family. How's Ann?"

"She's fine," Steph answered. "She'll meet us later."

"Great. Hey, it's lunch time. Let's go out. We can catch up." He glanced over at Mom to include her, but she shook her head.

"You kids go out."

I tried not to groan. "Okay." I really didn't have much of a choice. Steph beamed as she followed me out to the Jeep.

"Uh, Meg?"

"What?" I turned to face John.

"Don't you want a coat?"

I shut my eyes and sighed. "Yeah, I have one in the Jeep."

It didn't seem to make a whole lot of sense to him, but he let it slide.

"Do you want to drive?"

He smiled. "Nope, your Jeep now."

I grinned carefully and unlocked the jeep for everyone.

"We're glad you're home!" Steph bounced in her seat.

"It is nice to be home. The desert is barren. I miss green things."

"Not much green here this time of year," I said.

"More than the desert."

"So tell us about it." Steph buckled her seatbelt.

John shrugged, and I could smell his discomfort. "It's a lot of boring, with a very small amount of far-too-exciting," he finally said. "There really isn't much to tell. I mostly work at one of our base camps, so I'm not in much danger. Every once in a while, we get shot at, or I have to go out to one of our remote camps. Sometimes..." He trailed off, his expression going distant as if he were remembering things. Finally, he shook his head. "It's not important. I want to forget about it for a while."

"Fair enough." I knew how he felt, even though the circumstances were different.

"So, how are things here?"

Steph happily filled the rest of the drive with tales from high school. It wasn't terribly exciting, but it probably made John feel better. I even managed to throw in a story or two while I drove.

Predictably, we ended up at the Steak and Shake. It really was the only place to hang out, unless you could get into bars, and especially if you wanted food. There were plenty of restaurants, but they usually didn't encourage sitting around once you were done eating. I found a parking spot in the crowded lot and then followed Steph and John inside, wondering how I would get out of eating in front of John.

"Steph! Meg!"

I turned and sighed when I saw Gage. "Were we meeting them here?" I asked Steph quietly.

"Um, no."

John asked, "Friend of yours?"

"Yeah, kind of."

Gage waved us over to the large table.

John shrugged. "If I'm not cool enough to meet your friends..."

"Um, you're talking to the professionally uncool." Steph laughed.

John followed us over to Gage's table, selecting the seat next to me, and probably not incidentally, the seat that would give him the best view of the diner.

"Gage, this is my brother, John." I introduced them after a moment of awkward silence. "John, a friend of ours, Gage."

"Dude," Gage said enthusiastically. "Gary and Tad will be here in a bit. Where's Ann?"

I shrugged.

"I think she's out with Alexander. She'll meet us here after a while. I sent her a text." Steph waved her phone for emphasis.

"Great."

He seemed rather happy about something, but with my brother there, I suspected I wasn't going to find out what. John didn't need to know about our little Buffy-wannabe club. I hoped Gage had that figured out.

"I didn't know you had a brother," Gage said after a minute of uncomfortable silence.

"Yeah." I ignored John's upraised eyebrow. "Had one my whole life. He's in the army, and it never came up."

I was pretty sure he had joined the army, because he wanted to be a hero like our dad, and I really did consider him a true hero. Something I would never be. I pushed those depressing thoughts away, determined to enjoy myself.

Gage finally laughed. "Didn't know you had a sense of humor."

"Uh, I guess?"

John did look surprised at this. "Megan has a great sense of humor."

"I believe you. So, about Ann." Gage hesitated.

"Yes?" I frowned, wondering what he was talking about.

"Does she always talk like that?" Gage shifted uncomfortably.

"Talk like what?" Steph tilted her head, inviting an explanation.

"Well, you know, do not, and can not, and stuff. She never says don't, or, well, anything like that. It's weird," Gage said.

"Oh." We all laughed. "Yeah, awhile back she decided that contracting words was insulting to the words being contracted. It's her thing. Just go with it."

"Oh. Sure. Okay." Gage didn't really sound like he understood, but he let the subject drop.

I figured he'd fill in the others.

I caught a sense of Gary and Tad shortly before they entered the diner, and I had to fight the urge to jump up and warn them not to say anything in front of John. I also couldn't help but notice how Gary's infectious grin lit up his face even more than usual when he greeted Steph. I smiled, ignoring my jealousy, when Gary greeted me.

"New recruit?" Gary asked when he looked at John.

"No," I said too quickly, ignoring the questioning look from John. "This is my brother, John. He's on leave from the army. He didn't tell me he was coming home, so he could surprise me." I finished my explanation in a rush.

"New recruit to what?" Suspicion colored John's voice.

"Supernatural studies club," Tad said. "You're welcome to join, of course."

John's mouth gaped for a second before he snapped it shut. "Is that like studying witchcraft or something?"

"Uh...no." Gary sounded genuinely confused. "Well, I mean, witches are supernatural, so we might study them. History." He reached into Tad's backpack, glancing down for a moment before pulling a book out and sliding it across the table. *Werewolves Through Time* wasn't quite an accepted school textbook, but it had to be better than a witchcraft book.

"I see." John still sounded a little confused, but the spike of worry that had momentarily overwhelmed my nose subsided. "What gave you this idea?"

"Weird shit." Gage was nothing, if not eloquent.

Steph rolled her eyes. "We met at the library, of all places, and got talking. I dragged Meg and Ann in."

John seemed completely relieved, as if Steph would never lie to him.

"Excuse me. I have to use the restroom. Order my normal if they come by while I'm gone." Steph left the table.

I suspected she left so she could text Ann our new story.

"Oh, so, John, this is Gary and Tad. Sorry, I forgot."

"No problem."

Now that we had our "story" worked out, I was grateful that Gary, Tad, and Gage were there. With them around, John wouldn't bring up me sneaking out, if he did know. With John there, they wouldn't be able to bring up this morning's incident.

Whatever creature had killed the girl had made a mess, unlike the other murders. It had very obviously been targeting my victim, because there were plenty of people out on campus who would have been easier to get to. What the hell?

The waiter arrived, and I started to decline before I remembered John would think that was really strange. I had to order a burger and a shake, along with food for Steph, and we managed to make small talk until she returned a short time later.

"Well, don't let me interrupt your meeting. Feel free to carry on," John said.

Gary smiled. "We weren't actually intending on getting together, so we don't have anything planned. Just out for lunch."

Our food arrived, interrupting the line of questioning. A familiar, irritating feel washed over me, and I shuddered. "Ann's here," I grumbled.

John gave me a surprised look. "Don't sound so excited."

I shook my head and ground my teeth, fighting off the slimy feeling that touching Alexander's aura, or whatever it was I sensed, gave me.

"No, Meg is happy to see Ann. She doesn't like Ann's boyfriend," Steph explained.

"He's creepy." I growled.

Steph laughed. "Pot, kettle," she whispered.

John watched the door curiously and glanced at me again when Ann and her boyfriend walked in. Ann smiled brightly when she saw John and hurried forward to give him a hug.

"I'm so happy to see you." She grinned. Alexander followed hesitantly.

I refrained from glaring at him, mostly by pretending he wasn't there.

"Who's your friend?" John asked Ann once the initial greetings were over.

Ann blushed. I could smell the heat in her blood and quickly shut my eyes before they bled to black and caused a stir.

"This is Alexander." Ann sounded shy and uncertain.

The hint of vulnerability enhanced the delicious smell of her blood, and I finally stopped breathing so I wouldn't inhale any more of it.

"Are you okay?" Gary asked quietly while everyone else focused on Ann.

I nodded, not trusting myself to speak. Unfortunately, Alexander heard Gary.

"Yes, Megan. Are you okay?" He mocked.

I took a deep breath and got a hold of myself. I hoped my eyes were back to normal, and I opened them to glare at Alexander.

"Bite me, Alex." I put as much venom in my voice as I could.

"Too late." He laughed lightly.

I stood, more quickly than I had intended, and got in his face before anyone registered that I had moved. I made myself relax, met his eyes, and let all the anger I felt fall into my gaze. Alexander narrowed his intense blue eyes, and I could tell I had surprised him. I didn't do anything, just stared, and he finally took a step backward.

"I'll, um, see you later, Mary Ann," he stammered before turning and leaving.

I kept my eyes on him until he was outside. Finally I took a breath and returned to the table, pretending nothing odd had happened, despite the incredulous looks I received.

"Score one for the vampire," I muttered very quietly.

I shot a quick glance at Steph. She tried to hide a grin. Ann stared, flabbergasted, after her boyfriend, as did the guys. John frowned at me, apparently not sure what to do.

"Pot, kettle," Steph murmured, knowing I would hear.

I fought the urge to laugh, knowing it wouldn't go over well.

John finally asked, "So, what was that all about?"

"Alexander and Meg do not like each other." Ann sounded shaken, but not angry. I had expected anger.

"Is there any reason?" I suspected John guessed jealousy.

"Yeah, he's creepy, like not even human," I said before I could stop myself.

Ann looked at me, eyes shocked. "So are you!"

"Umm."

She sat down in the empty chair and stole my plate. She made it seem like it was in anger, but I knew she was doing me a favor.

"That's not the only reason I don't like him, Ann. He, like, tries to eat my soul every time he looks at me. That is a bit creepy."

"Really? Cool." Ann grinned.

I hid my face with my hand for a minute, trying to decide if I should laugh or cry. I finally settled on laughing.

"Now that we have that out of the way, do you want what is left of my shake?"

"Yes."

I slid it across to Ann, hoping no one noticed I hadn't really touched it. The diner gave you the milkshake in a glass, but they also gave you the rest of it in the stainless steel container it was mixed in. I had managed to dump some of it back in there while everyone was distracted.

Steph was the only other person at the table who knew the full story, and only she looked concerned. Everyone else was very obviously confused as hell.

We had a few moments of peace before the screaming started.

Chapter 15

It took me a moment to react, thinking the panicked wail might be in my head.

The horrified expressions on the others' faces convinced me it wasn't. I shoved my chair back and ran for the parking lot, trying to keep to a semi-normal, human speed. John followed close on my heels.

I stopped after pushing my way through the small crowd that had gathered around the fallen girl and stared at her, amazed at how familiar she seemed. I knew I'd never been around her before, or at least never smelled her blood, which now seeped from her slit neck into her clothing and pooled around her. I looked up, glancing quickly around. Alexander stared at the girl, and I thought I saw a quick flash of shock before his face smoothed into his normal, impassive, arrogant state.

He looked up and met my eyes before staring back at the girl. Her plump frame and mousy brown hair were very similar to Ann's. Her face was different, but not remarkably so, and someone who didn't know her well could have mistaken her for Ann from a distance. I went cold, hoping Ann didn't notice the similarity. That made any desire I felt for the blood leaking from the girl's neck go away.

"Did you hear any screaming this time?" Tad asked quietly, joining me.

I had to think for a minute before I understood what he meant, the shock of the dead girl slowing my mind. I shook my head. "Nothing you didn't hear." I looked again at Alexander. He met my eyes again before backing away, melting out of the growing crowd. Sirens blared in the distance.

I really wanted to talk to Alexander, certain he knew more than he let on about the murders. Unfortunately, before I could chase after him, John put his arm around me and backed me out of the crowd.

"You don't need to see that," he said.

"Too late," I muttered. "Damn. Now Mom is never going to let us out of the house."

John glared at me, opening his mouth as if to chastise me for my callousness, but then he shook his head and remained quiet. Ann, Steph, and the guys joined us. I fought another flash of jealousy as Gary put his arm around Steph.

We spent the next hour being interviewed by the cops. Then we were allowed to leave once they searched the Jeep for the murderer or something. I already knew they weren't going to find it. Whatever the creature was, it probably wasn't human and was long gone–I was convinced of that now.

When John and I got home, Mom broke down sobbing. We finally got her to calm down, and I got out of dinner by saying I wasn't hungry. They let me slip off to my room, and I used the excuse of homework to remain antisocial until Mom went to bed.

"Meg?" John said softly, knocking on my door.

"I'm awake."

"Will you be all right?" He pushed the door open and came inside, sitting on my desk chair.

"Yeah. I'm fine."

"You sure?"

I snorted. "We've had plenty of dead people around here recently."

"This is the first one you've seen though." It was almost, but not quite, a question.

I shrugged. "Maybe I'm in shock. I don't know, but I feel fine."

"Good. So you're…" He hesitated. "You're not going to sneak out tonight, are you?"

I just looked at him.

"Meg, I'm not going to tell Mom. I did plenty of sneaking out when I was your age."

"You did?" His confession genuinely surprised me. I hadn't realized he'd done that.

"Yeah, but really, stay in until this guy is caught."

If only it were that easy. I really wanted to tell him what was going on. Maybe he could even help, but when I opened my mouth to speak, I couldn't get the words to come out. He wouldn't believe me, or worse, if he did, he'd be horrified. I wasn't sure how Steph and Ann dealt, but I couldn't expect my luck to hold out.

"Meg, I don't want to see you like that," he said when he didn't get agreement from me.

"I'm not sneaking out at night." I added power to my voice. "I'm fine. Don't worry about me."

I wasn't sure how successful I was, but John didn't bring it up again. He said goodnight after a few more minutes. I waited until he went to his room, then got up and locked the door. Ugh. I wouldn't have been sneaking out at all if I'd had any choice.

Unfortunately, my prediction that Mom wasn't about to let us go anywhere was correct. I was almost okay with it, though I had started to enjoy our meetings with the guys. At the same time, at least I didn't have to deal with the discomfort of discussing vampires and things around them. Or so I thought.

"She's not going to let me out of the house," I said to Steph on the phone. "Why can't they just email us?"

"Just try. And it's fun to hang out. Besides, you can convince her."

I shook my head, not wanting to use my new powers against my mom if I didn't have to.

"I'm sure she'll let you come over here. Ann is on her way, and the guys have stuff they want to share."

"I'll try." I hesitated. "I'm guessing I'll have to bring John along."

"That's fine. He might be able to help."

"Okay," I said after a longer pause. "I'll try."

I grabbed my backpack and headed downstairs.

"Hey, Mom. Can I go to Steph's house?"

I could feel her object before she even opened her mouth to say no.

"Um, it's Steph's house. Why not?"

"Because it isn't safe."

"If I'm not safe there, I'm certainly not safe here."

Mom shook her head, not even willing to be reasonable.

"That doesn't make any sense." I cringed inwardly at the hint of a whine. I considered getting over it and using mind control on her.

"I'll go with her." John broke the stubborn silence.

Mom folded her arms.

"Mom. There is no reason to keep Meg locked up here. She's going to have to go to school tomorrow."

Mom angrily shook her head. "Fine, whatever. You go with her." She turned and left the room.

I shared a look with John before rolling my eyes. "You're welcome to come."

"That's probably a good thing." He grabbed his jacket.

I remembered to grab one as well and shot Steph a quick text letting her know I'd be over. I wasn't sure how we were going to convince John that we weren't crazy. I guess I'd let Steph handle it. She was the master of convincing.

I parked in the driveway, noting the presence of Gage's battered pickup. Steph met us at the door, blushing slightly when she smiled at John. I rolled my eyes and followed her into the basement.

"Your parents aren't wondering about the guys?" I asked when we were in the stairwell.

She shook her head. "No, I told them we were a study group."

"I'm getting the impression you're not a study group then?" John asked carefully.

"Yeah, we are," Steph said after a moment of consideration. "Someone has to be prepared."

"For what?"

"You don't think all these murders around here are normal, do you?"

"Um, well, the last time we had any violent crime, besides a bar fight, was about twenty years ago, so no. They aren't normal."

"Exactly. Some supernatural baddie is going around killing people."

She said it matter-of-factly and kept walking, even when John stopped on the stairs. I could feel the shock and worry course through him, colored with a delicious tinge of fear. I growled and stalked down the stairs after Steph.

"'Supernatural baddie?'" I said when I caught up to Steph in the downstairs living room. Gary and Gage looked up from some papers on the coffee table.

"What else do you want me to call the creature that is doing the killing? We don't know what it is. It isn't a vampire, and it's probably not some sort of werewolf."

"What makes you think it's supernatural?" John finally followed us into the room.

"Hi, John." Gary put the paper he was reading on the table.

Tad barely looked up from staring intently at his laptop, and Gage waved briefly before looking back at the paper in his hands.

"What else could it be?"

"Umm, Steph, there are plenty of logical explanations that don't involve vampires and ghosts. They don't exist," John said.

I sank into the comfortable armchair.

"Yes, they do," Steph replied.

"Oh, hard to argue logic like that," I muttered.

"Don't tell me you believe this, Megan?" John folded his arms across his chest.

I cringed inwardly. He hadn't called me by my full name in quite some time. Ever since Ann, Steph, and I had decided it was cool to shorten our names back when we were six. It had stuck.

"It's hard not to, really." I had no good answer as to why I believed. I couldn't very well tell him I was a vampire.

"Dude, just look at this stuff." Gage thrust a handful of papers at John.

John gave him a wary look before accepting them. He didn't look at them though, but simply stared at Gary.

"Whose idea was this, anyway?"

Tad and Steph both raised their hands.

"We thought of it separately, but ran into each other and joined forces."

John seemed shocked. "Um." He finally sank onto the couch.

"Read that while we chat."

"So, Tad has news." Gage leaned back in his chair. "He thinks this wacko is some sort of Fae."

"Like a Faerie?" I asked.

"Kind of. More like the Seelie and Unseelie courts," Tad said, managing to get a word in.

I gave him a blank stare.

"The Unseelie are the really nasty ones, and the Seelie are slightly nicer, or at least more human from what I've been able to determine. All the really vicious ones belong to the

Unseelie court. So I'm guessing we're dealing with some sort of Unseelie Fae."

"Uh." That was almost too much, even for me. I had to believe in vampires, but I couldn't help picturing Tinker Bell flying around and sprinkling faerie dust on the people that had been killed. I snorted.

Obviously, Tad could tell I didn't believe him.

"I'm serious. Read this." He thrust an old book at me.

"'Banshee, a type of Fae that wails before a member of certain Irish clans die.' Um, Tad? Banshee?"

"Despite Chelsea's Aryan good looks, she was of Irish descent."

"Okay. So a German-looking, Irish sorority girl gets killed, and I'm the only one that hears the banshee wail?"

Tad shrugged.

"All right, fine. But this doesn't say that banshee kill people. So we're not dealing with a banshee. And I'm not a member of her family."

"Right. That was just a start. So we have a banshee that apparently you can hear, even though you're not family, and we have something going around that was killing mysteriously, but is now slitting throats. The first victims have no apparent cause of death, though were somewhat low on blood. Now the victims are low on blood and have their throats slit. The last few deaths would be more easily explained by a human killer, except no one saw anything, and they were surrounded by people at the time.

"It was daytime, so that rules out vampires. The other deaths have been early in the mornings, so it could have been a vampire, but there were no fang marks. No other type of supernatural creature I have been able to research kills like that. So it leaves Fae."

"I think your logic has some holes," I grumbled. I couldn't tell him that vampires didn't leave marks. The wounds healed when I was done feeding, though I didn't know why.

"So it's not perfect," he said defensively. "Do you have any better ideas?"

John asked, "Why is it so hard to believe it might be a human?"

"No one saw anything, in the middle of the day. Well, it was getting on toward evening, but still. There have been no connections between the victims, except that they happened to be out and about at the wrong time of day. Human killers usually have a pattern." Tad leaned back in his chair and glared at John.

"I would think supernatural killers would have patterns, too." John crossed his arms and glared right back.

"Maybe."

I couldn't share the connection between the victims with him. I wasn't sure why she'd been killed, if it wasn't because she looked so much like Ann.

I heard the now familiar sound of Alexander's car. "Ann's here."

The guys stared at me.

"What?"

"How?" Gage asked suspiciously.

Steph came to my defense. "It's Meg's superpower. She's good at identifying cars by sound."

I stared after her as she walked up the stairs. My superpower? Right....

Chapter 16

"So don't tell me you're in on this, too," John said when Ann joined us.

"Alexander had a few thoughts." Ann ignored John. "He brought it up, not me."

"Oh?"

"Well, yeah." Ann shrugged. "He does not know about our group." She turned her hazel eyes, currently a stormy gray, on me, as if trying to tell me Alexander knew what I was.

I nodded. I already knew that.

"Or rather he does not know what we're doing. Obviously, he has seen us together several times."

"Yeah." I shivered, remembering how his eyes tried to eat me.

"He thinks it may be some sort of, um, Faerie."

"How would he know anything?" Gage frowned.

Ann shrugged. "I do not know."

"Maybe we should add Alexander to our group?" Gary suggested tentatively.

"No!" I protested.

"Okay," Tad said into the increasingly uncomfortable silence. "Since we have two people who believe this is a Fae, and no one else has any better ideas..." He looked at me for a moment and continued when I didn't say anything. "I think we need to figure out what their weaknesses are. I've done a little research, and the only thing that my sources agree on is that they don't like cold iron. It burns them, or something. Maybe like what holy water is supposed to do to a vampire."

I shuddered. We hadn't tested holy water yet, though the cross hadn't bothered me. Maybe you had to be a religious vampire.

"We need to find some cold iron then," Gary said.

Ann rummaged in her purse.

"Alexander gave me these for everyone. He, uh, said they might help. I bet they are cold iron." She held out what looked like tiny bike chains, links of dull metal in small loops. "There is one for everyone."

"Did he touch them?" I asked before I could help myself.

Steph took one of the loops of metal and studied it, turning it over in her hand.

"Umm."

"Ann, did he touch them?"

"No, they were on the counter." She frowned as she tried to remember.

"Hmm…" I took the chain she held out to me. It tingled mildly when I touched it, and I had to resist the urge to put it down.

"He said they might help keep us safe," she said uncertainly.

Alexander had even thoughtfully provided one for John. I stared at mine suspiciously, while Ann showed Steph how to open it. Steph put it on like a necklace. I bristled at the idea of anything of Alexander's coming anywhere near my neck, especially if he was one of the Fae.

"Aren't you not supposed to accept gifts from Faeries?" I put the necklace on the table.

I felt all the eyes in the room zero in on me; the silence profound.

"What is that supposed to mean?" Ann finally said.

"I told you I didn't think he was human."

Ann's expression turned inward as if she were considering something. "He is just as human as you are," she said a little hotly.

My jaw dropped. Damn her, anyway.

"Meg, you're gonna catch flies here in a minute." I could hear the low note of warning in Steph's voice. "Okay. So now that we have that out of our system." Steph touched the chain. "Even if we shouldn't accept gifts from Faeries, Ann isn't a Fae, and I accepted this from her. So it's fine."

"Great," I muttered, "So Ann gets to bear the full burden." But I said it quietly enough that no one would hear.

The guys slipped on their chains, and even John finally did as well.

"Am I the only one that thinks this is a bad idea?"

A dozen scenarios flashed through my mind–enchanted necklaces that bound us to their maker; a slow poison that leached out of the metal, killing the wearer; an un-repayable debt to the Fae...

"Meg, it is cold iron. The Seelie and Unseelie cannot enchant, affect, or otherwise do anything with it. Put it on."

I glared at Ann, wondering how she suddenly knew so much.

"Fine. But if your boyfriend has done anything to these that is harmful, I'm personally going to tear his throat out."

"Meg, that was uncalled for," John said sternly.

I snorted. "I sure hope so." The metal felt cool against my skin as it settled around my neck. I felt a slight tingle before it warmed to match my slightly-above-room-temperature skin.

"It tingles."

"Alexander said you might feel that, but it will not hurt you. You are my friends, and he wants to try and help protect you."

I had a feeling that comment was directed specifically at me, though she tried to include the whole room when she spoke.

"Fine. So, cold iron. Anything else?"

Ann shrugged.

"Great. So how are we supposed to stop the killer?"

"You aren't. That's a job for the cops." John glared at me.

I laughed. I couldn't help it. "Yeah, I can see that call now. "Yes, officer, there is this Unseelie Faerie running around murdering people. You have to kill him with cold iron.'"

John shut his eyes, and I could sense his irritation, the heat of his blood spiking, tang of anger hinting the air.

"I'm sorry, John, but seriously. We know it isn't a human doing this. I don't think the authorities are up to the task."

"And what makes you think you are?"

"Well, we have Gage and his shotgun, Tad and his computer, Gary with his nice smile,"–I blushed–"Ann with her creepy Faerie boyfriend, Steph and her way with words, and my superpower to identify cars by sound from well-insulated basements. Oh, and we've all seen a lot of Buffy. I think we have it covered. Want to join us?"

"You're a lot more cynical than you were when I left."

I shrugged. "It's been a rough few months. Do you want to help us?"

John seemed surprised that I asked him again. He glanced around at everyone else, who shrugged or nodded.

"Fine, but only to keep you out of trouble." It seemed obvious, even without my extra senses, that John was humoring us.

"Great. We need to start looking for our bad guy then. I have been, but I haven't seen anything."

"We have been as well. The murder on campus was the closest we've come to the killer, and again, no one saw anything," Tad said.

"Maybe we should go out now," I suggested.

"Sure. Why not?" John tried for a light tone, but the irritation still came through.

"Cool. I like hunting." I stood and, to my surprise, everyone followed suit. The day was looking up.

We walked through one of the parks close to the college. The scattered trees, thinner in the park than in the surrounding forest, sprinkled snow down on us periodically as we walked. The air had the peaceful, deadened quality common in the winter, and I felt grateful for the semblance of normalcy as we hiked.

There were other tracks in the snow, crisscrossing each other–some human, some the smaller tracks of squirrels and the few birds that hadn't flown south for the winter. There were some larger deer tracks, and a few dog tracks matched with the humans. The snow went ankle deep, but not so deep that you couldn't enjoy the park.

Ann turned to my brother. "How long are you here for?"

"I'm here through Christmas. I got lucky this year."

I wasn't looking forward to the holiday break. It would mean more time I had to spend avoiding my mom. With everything else, I'd forgotten about it.

"Anything?" Steph asked as we finished circling the park.

I knew she directed the question at me, since I was the most likely to sense something odd. Right now, we were trying to find traces of our killer or maybe a secret hideout or something. We had no idea what we were doing, but it was better than sitting around doing nothing. It was dark when we finally conceded defeat for the day. Everyone, except me, shivered, wet from the snow.

"Hot chocolate at my house, then we can try again tomorrow." Steph sounded far too cheerful.

Chapter 17

"I wanted to know if you two would go dress shopping with me?" Ann asked in a rush the next day at school.

"Dress shopping?" I had thought it would be something–I don't know–more serious.

"Yeah. I'm taking Alexander to the winter dance, and I need a dress. I don't actually have a formal."

"Oh."

"Sure!" Steph grinned. She was the only one of us who had actually been asked to a dance before, though the three of us always went to homecoming together if we didn't have dates, which was every year but one.

"Yeah, sounds like fun." I did my best to sound enthusiastic.

Steph blushed. "I was thinking about asking Gary," she whispered after a minute.

Ann giggled. I tried to be happy for my friends, I really did, but I wanted a normal life, too.

"Does he have a girlfriend?"

"No," she replied.

I smiled. "Then ask him. He's nice, and he likes you."

Steph stared at me. "How do you know?"

"Duh, it's obvious."

"He smiles every time he sees you." Ann giggled.

"Then I will."

"That means you'll need a dress, too."

Steph considered for a moment, tilting her head as if she was taking a mental inventory of her closet.

"Yeah, I guess I will."

They both looked at me.

"What?"

"Anyone you're going to ask?" Steph asked me.

"You're joking, right?"

"Why not?"

"First off, who would I ask? I've avoided my male friends all year, and it would kind of suck if they tried to kiss me, and really, who would I ask?" I paused. "I guess I could take John."

Steph laughed. "I'll ask Gary if he wants to go with you, and I'll take John, and we can share."

"Uh. No, really, that's okay. You take Gary. I'll see if John wants to go. It'll be fine."

"Great. We'll go shopping after school."

"Fine." I smiled at Steph. "But you get to convince Mom to let me go."

Steph grinned. "Sure." She pulled out her phone.

I tried to take notes as Steph worked her magic on my mom, but finally I came to the conclusion that I would have to use mind control to accomplish the things Steph sweet-talked her way into. It was quite the superpower.

After she spoke to Mom, she sent off a quick text, and the response left her grinning.

"I think that's cheating." I smiled, standing as the bell for class rang.

"What?" She failed to sound innocent.

"Asking Gary out over text."

"I didn't ask him to date me, just to go to the dance. It's different."

"Oh, I see." I rolled my eyes at her, and she smiled back.

I managed to keep up the illusion of happiness until I got to class. Then, I slouched in my chair and tried not to glare at the teacher, while I fought off my jealousy.

I had recovered by the time school finished for the day, and I met my friends by the back door.

"Gary wants to know if you have a date," Steph said when we got into the Jeep.

"Why?"

"I didn't ask."

"Right." Somehow I didn't believe her. The engine growled to life, and I let it warm up before I risked the chaos of the student parking lot. "What did you tell him?" I backed out, cutting off several people as I did so. No one stopped to let you out in the student parking lot.

"Haven't had time to reply yet."

"Ah. Well you know the answer to that question." I tried to ignore the empty pit in my stomach, in turn, hungry and depressed.

Ann and Steph kept up a cheerful banter the whole way to the mall. There were only a handful of places people could shop around us, unless you had a lot of money to spend, and none of us could afford expensive dresses. But there were a couple of stores in the mall itself, and we knew about a used clothing store not too far away.

I followed after Steph and Ann, letting their happy chatter distract me.

Steph occasionally handed me a dress, and I held them absently as I followed her and Ann toward a dressing room. I wasn't exactly lost in thought, but I wasn't able to focus on what they were doing. It was as if something pulled at my attention.

"Meg?"

"What?" I jerked myself back from wherever I was and tried to focus on my friends.

"Are you going to try those on?"

I glanced at Steph and then at the dresses in my hand. "Uh, sure."

"Good. Make sure you show us."

I rolled my eyes. "Maybe we should take turns."

"We are," Ann said. "You get to go first."

"Why do I have to go first?"

"Because you were off in la-la land when we decided."

"Great. Thanks."

I let myself into the changing stall and looked at the dresses Steph had chosen.

I wasn't sure I liked the styles this year, but whatever. I showed off the dresses with inconclusive results and tried hard to pay more attention when Steph and Ann tried on theirs, mostly managing to succeed.

"What's up?" Steph asked as we walked to the next store.

"I don't know. It's like something is pulling at my attention. It's weird."

Steph frowned, looking around the mall curiously. "I don't sense anything."

"That's probably good."

We wove through the horrible perfume section of a second store. I was amazed I made it out with my ability to smell intact.

I didn't like any of the dresses in the second store either, but we found a deep green one Steph really liked with a flowing skirt and thin straps. I thought it would look good on her, setting off her strawberry blonde hair.

They were still chatting happily as I led them to the Jeep. The strange feeling that had been nagging me the entire trip came back, drawing my attention across the parking lot. I stopped, barely noticing when Ann collided with my back. I felt like I pushed through a dense fog, but I knew something was over there. Something that didn't want to be seen.

"Get the Jeep warmed up," I said, handing the keys to Steph. Then I dashed across the parking lot, hoping I wouldn't be seen.

A slightly plump girl with mousy brown hair walked to a car. She was a little shorter than Ann, but still, the similarity was notable. She walked slowly, looking around her, the sour smell of worry coloring her scent. I didn't see anyone else, though I felt her unease was probably justified.

She held a shopping bag tightly in her one hand, keys clutched in the other, ready to put in the lock. Her eyes darted about, and I could hear her heart racing, taste the blood rushing through her veins.

I crouched down next to a black sedan, the tick of the cooling engine loud as I stretched out all my senses, trying to find the source of the danger. I could only sense a slight concentration of the feeling of "don't look here." It rapidly approached the girl.

I ran toward her. Anger filled the air around me. My plan had been to try and talk to her, but whatever it was knew I had seen it. And it wanted blood. I threw up my arm as a shield and ran into her.

The girl shrieked, dropping her shopping bag, and something shattered.

I pulled her to the ground, barely registering the sharp pain across my forearm, though the coppery scent of blood did get my attention. After a moment of panic, I realized it was my own, not the girl's.

"What are you doing!"

"Sorry, tripped," I muttered, looking around, hoping we were safe.

Fury washed around me, impotent but frightening. The girl's screams had attracted attention, and other shoppers were running toward us. Blood splashed to the ground. I could hear it drip, feel it flow from my arm. I felt dizzy. I tried to stop the bleeding, but it continued to pour from the deep wound, soaking my jacket and pooling on the ground.

The world around me grew distant, and then hands were tugging at me, pulling me away from the girl and shoving me against a tree.

"What the hell do you think you're doing?"

I tried to meet his electric blue eyes, but my vision wouldn't focus. Alexander swore. "Stay here. I'll be right back."

Rough bark tugged at my jacket and caught my hair as I sank to the ground, leaning against a tree, exhausted, the world wavering around me.

Chapter 18

Someone grabbed me, helping me to a car. I didn't struggle, mostly because I didn't have the energy. I vaguely heard someone talking on a phone, telling the other person to meet somewhere. Then I must have passed out, because I woke with my teeth buried in someone's wrist. Hot, sweet, oddly spicy blood poured into my mouth.

I groaned.

"Meg," someone said.

A hand touched my shoulder, and the jolt that went through me brought me to my senses. I released the wrist and clamped my mouth shut, not sure I wanted to know what was going on.

"Is she okay?"

"Yes."

"What?" I couldn't bring myself to say more.

"You, rather foolishly, saved a girl's life," Alexander said.

I stared at him, meeting his blue eyes. I vaguely remembered him pulling me away from someone, telling me to stay put.

"What?"

Alexander shut his eyes, an exasperated expression crossing his features.

"You managed to prevent the killer from murdering someone, which in the short term is good, but quite honestly, is really going to piss him off. I expect he'll try and retaliate."

"Oh." I looked around, not needing to ask where I lay, now that I could focus. I was in Alexander's kitchen, lying on his island countertop. The blinds were closed. Someone, probably Alexander, had ripped the sleeve of my shirt away, and dark red bandages coated my arm. I could smell something pungent and wondered if he'd applied a salve.

If there had been any question in my mind before, it was obvious he knew I was a vampire.

"What happened to me?"

"You took the blow intended for the girl across your arm. Unfortunately, the weapon was enchanted. You couldn't heal the wound, and it went very deep. I managed to get the bleeding stopped."

He didn't mention anything about giving me blood, and I wasn't comfortable enough to mention it either.

"What were you doing there?" The weakness faded quickly, but I didn't feel good enough to try sitting up yet.

Ann and Steph came to my other side. Steph put her hand hesitantly on my arm.

"Hunting," he said wryly. "Of course, somehow you managed to see what I couldn't. How did you find him?"

"I looked for the greatest concentration of 'don't look here,' and found it chasing a girl."

Alexander looked thoughtful. Ann and Steph looked confused. Of course, Alexander said he'd been hunting, but I wasn't completely sure I believed him. He had likely saved my life, and unfortunately, now I owed him.

"Okay, I'm going to attempt sitting up."

Alexander stepped back, and I carefully rolled to my side and swung my legs over the edge. I took it as a good sign that the world didn't spin and decided to try standing. My legs supported my weight, and I started to feel really good.

"I guess I should say thank you." I met Alexander's vibrant blue eyes again.

He nodded. "You are welcome. Despite your condition, you do seem to be trying to help."

"What the hell is that supposed to mean?"

He actually smiled. "You're a vampire. Sort of. My kind and yours don't get along as a general rule."

"And you're what, some sort of Faerie?" Visions of Tinker Bell dancing around forced me to stifle a laugh.

Alexander managed not to look horribly offended, though I could sense his annoyance, as if his emotions echoed inside of me. I used to have a hard time reading him, but now, it felt like he was an open book, and he was amused, despite his annoyance.

"No. Well, yes, but no. My mother is human. My father, a lesser member of the Seelie courts." He stopped, wanting to know if I understood.

"Yes. I understand. Kind of. Um, why can I read you now? I couldn't before." Alexander looked away and ran his hand through his dark hair nervously.

"It will fade, but not entirely. Yet another reason why our kind don't get along."

I stared at him for a minute. So I could read his mind now? Or his surface thoughts anyway. And I'd always be able to. Huh. At least, now I knew he wasn't the killer. I wondered if the connection went both ways. I did not want Faerie boy in my head.

"I would appreciate it if you wouldn't mention what I did to anyone. It could get me into trouble."

"Thank you." I could feel how much admitting it cost him, so I kept my snide remarks to myself.

"We should get going," Steph finally said. "I told your mom we were stopping for coffee, but we are still running later than we should."

I looked at myself again, dismayed at the state my clothes were in. "Damn."

"I will burn your clothes."

"Uh, sure…"

"Give me your shirt. I will do it before you leave. I have another you can wear, and you can clean up in the bathroom."

I hesitated slightly before pulling off my shirt. He barely looked at me before gathering my ruined winter coat and taking them to the fireplace.

"Here." Ann handed me my cold iron necklace.

I settled it around my neck and went to the bathroom to clean up. The sight greeting me in the mirror was both better and worse than I had imagined. My face wasn't covered with Alexander's blood, though some of it had smeared on my chin and the side of my mouth. Blood coated one side of my dark jeans, but my winter coat had obviously absorbed most of it, because the stains weren't terribly bad. My stomach and chest were also coated in my own blood, and I took my time scrubbing at them with a spare cloth.

Steph knocked on the door quietly and handed me a shirt when I opened it.

"Thanks."

"Sure. You're okay?"

"I think so, yeah." Tremors of fear ran down my spine, but she didn't need to know that.

"Cool."

I shut the door and put on the shirt, trying to avoid staring at myself in the mirror.

"You can take those off when you get home." Alexander pointed to the bandages when I left the bathroom.

"All right." I held out the cloth, and he took it back to the fireplace.

"And you should be fine by tomorrow," he added, returning.

"Thanks."

He gave Ann a quick hug as we left his house. I could sense his unease–he had noted the similarity between the victims and Ann, as well.

"Okay, that was intense," Steph said once we were outside.

"Do you see now why I think your plan to fight supernatural crime is a bad one? I just got my ass kicked, and I'm the indestructible one."

Steph flinched at the angry tone in my voice.

Ann defended Steph. "Meg, lighten up."

"Sorry. I just don't want you guys to get hurt. Oh, and you don't seem very surprised that Alexander is a half-Seelie."

Ann smiled a little. "He told me, but I have not had time to tell you guys yet. The mall was not a good place to bring it up."

"Okay," Steph said. "So, we have to be more careful. But you did save that girl's life, so we're doing something good."

Steph. Ever the optimist.

"Megan," a voice whispered.

I looked up from the homework I slogged through.

"Meg," the voice whispered again.

I looked around my bedroom, certain I was alone. The voice sounded familiar, bringing an image of shocking blue eyes and the hint of spicy blood.

"Alexander?" I said softly.

"Hunt with me?"

I sighed. "Don't you hate me?" I muttered as I quickly finished the paragraph I'd been working on for English class.

The quiet voice laughed.

I put my books away and quietly locked my door. Just to be sure, I wedged a chair under the knob before walking to my window.

I didn't see Alexander, but I knew he waited close by under a clump of pine trees. I could smell the sweet scent of sap, even though I was nowhere near him. Fear sent shivers down my spine, and I rubbed my arms, fighting off an imaginary chill. Alexander said our link would fade with time. I hoped he was right, because I didn't like having direct access to his mind.

Since I couldn't afford to lose another jacket, I went for a plain white shirt no one would miss if I destroyed it and an old pair of jeans. My arm wasn't completely healed, but it was close. A few thin scars traced along my pale skin.

I climbed out my window onto the narrow ledge and slid it shut. Most of the snow had melted from the roof, so I didn't have to cover my tracks, but it still presented a problem on the ground. I hadn't figured out how to get around it other than jumping from underneath my window to the shoveled walk. It was a good ten feet, but I could make it from a standing jump.

Low, heavy clouds reflected light off the dirty snow. The air was still, and the sharp, cold scent of snow permeated the night. I guessed we were going to get another storm soon, maybe even tonight.

I hurried away from my house, some sense allowing me to head unerringly toward the trees hiding Alexander. I saw a faint shimmer around him–glamour shielding him from the casual observer. His head tilted forward, and his dark hair had fallen into his eyes. It was cute.

"I don't hate you," he said softly as I approached. "I did save your life."

I arched an eyebrow at him.

"Well, I did that for Ann, but you're obviously trying to help."

"I see." I could smell the rich scent of his blood now that I was closer, almost feel it, as his heart pushed it through his veins. I ground my teeth and tore my eyes away from his throat.

"That is another reason your kind and mine don't get along." He looked uncomfortable. "Our blood is potent, and your kind tends to regard it as a delicacy."

I sighed. "Sorry. So, any idea where this guy might be?"

"I have a few thoughts, but so far, I've been unable to find him. Perhaps you can see through his magic where I can't."

"Okay. But I have to be home before it's time to go to school."

Alexander tried, unsuccessfully, to hide a smirk. "Very well."

I decided to refrain from punching him, but only because I wanted to stop the killer, too.

"So, what do I need to know?"

Alexander hesitated, and I could feel the thoughts whirling around in his head, too fast for me to follow. The one thing I did get was a picture of a man, stooped, disturbing to look at, as if his proportions were a touch off, arms just a bit too long and legs a bit too short. Not something you would notice if you were looking at him sitting down, but seen together, it made your eyes water. His hair was stringy, long in places, but patchy and dirty-dishwater blond with hints of green. His forehead jutted out thickly over his deep-set eyes, but he had a small nose, and a weak chin.

"That's what we're looking for?" I tried to keep the horror out of my voice.

"Yeah, or near enough, anyway."

"What?"

"He has powerful glamour. He's of the Unseelie court. Therefore, he can make almost anyone see whatever he wants them to. This is as close to what we can figure his true form actually is."

"Oh."

He led me at a brisk walk away from the house. I followed, senses on full, wary of ambush. I had felt the anger of the creature we sought yesterday before I'd blacked out, and it had been frightening enough then. I didn't want to face it full on.

"How do we kill it?"

Alexander gave me a look I couldn't quite interpret, though I could sense his frustration, bordering on anger.

"What? Obviously we have to kill it."

"I'm not sure we can. We have to find and contain it. If we can, then others will come to take him away."

I stopped.

He turned to face me.

"He's a murderer. If he gets out, he'll do it again. And I'm guessing he'll have a long memory, and in theory, I'm going to live a long time. I don't want him showing up on my doorstep one day, pissed off because I got him thrown in Tinker Bell prison."

Alexander's jaw dropped, and I heard him repeat my last words in his head.

Tinker Bell prison?

I was serious, despite my flippant words.

Alexander worked his jaw for a few moments, before he finally got something to come out. "What?"

"You heard me." I started walking again.

"Really, I don't actually think we can kill him. It's not that I don't want to, though there would be political repercussions that I'm not sure I'm up to dealing with if we did. Two considerations: one, if we can kill him, the other Unseelie might decide we are dangerous, and then they might decide to kill us; two, if we try and fail, he's going to be even more upset than he is now."

I shrugged, scuffing my feet on the concrete sidewalk.

"Meg. There are rules to living in the supernatural world. If you don't follow them, it could get you killed."

"I can't follow the rules if I don't know them. And if you hadn't noticed, no one bothered to stick around and fill me in. Oh, and while we're on the subject–what did you mean when you said I was 'kind of' a vampire?" I looked at him again.

"Well, you can go out in the sunlight. I've never met a vampire who could." Alexander glanced at me.

"I can't do direct sunlight."

"Interesting."

"So, you don't actually know anything other than that I'm weird and can go out during the day?"

"Well, no."

I shook my head. "Okay. Fine. How do we contain Tinker Bell?"

"I wouldn't let him hear you call him that."

"I'm shaking in my boots."

"Megan, I'm serious."

I shrugged. "Really, my life is pretty much done as far as being normal. What else can he do to me? Kill me? I walked away oncc; maybc I'll be able to do it again. If not, at least I won't be living off of humans anymore." Even I was surprised at how bitter I sounded.

Alexander remained quiet for a while, and I could tell he was trying to keep his thoughts from me. I didn't listen, just followed him as he led me toward the industrial part of town. In our town, industrial meant the one factory that produced some pharmaceuticals and employed about a quarter of the community, and several abandoned warehouses. What little crime we did have seemed to involve tagging the warehouses and minor vandalism on the edge of the historic downtown.

"I can probably teach you some, but it will be different for you. Vampire society is more lethal. The Sidhe are not less dangerous, just less quick to kill. There are plenty of other things they can do to make your life miserable. Death is too easy. Vampires, well...they are killers. That's what they do. Staying alive is a complicated dance through politics."

"Oh." I wondered again about the one who had turned me. I considered asking Alexander, but really, I just didn't know him that well.

"Which I'm guessing you're not good at."

"Um, seriously, I'm a high school student. When would I ever learn that?" Alexander shook his head. "Even high school has its political maneuverings. I suggest you start to learn."

"Right."

"It could save your life."

I refrained from more bitter or sarcastic remarks. Go me. Maybe that was a step in learning how to stay alive. Then again, maybe not.

Chapter 19

The warehouse district seemed darker, with less snow, more dirt, and fewer lights.

The factory stood as a glowing beacon amongst the dark warehouses. Alexander led me toward the abandoned buildings. If I hadn't had a direct line to his thoughts and if he hadn't already saved my life, I probably wouldn't have followed him, vampire or not.

"What's out here?"

"It's one of the places I haven't checked yet. I wanted backup. It's empty, remote, but close enough to town to be convenient. And there is enough iron in the buildings that most Sidhe will stay away. A good place to hide if you can deal with the discomfort. I don't think our Unseelie cares much about being a little uncomfortable."

“How come you didn’t ask your other friends?”

“What other friends?”

“Jennifer and Candice.”

“Who?”

“Wait, you don’t know Ann’s other new friends?”

“Oh, those two. I guess I don’t really know them. Ann has mentioned them a few times though. I did suggest to her, at one point, that she start hanging out with more than two other people. I guess those are the two she picked.”

“Oh. Why?”

“I didn’t know how she’d feel about finding out you were a vampire. I could tell she didn’t know, and I didn’t want her to be completely without friends if you freaked her out too much."

I mulled that over for a while. It sort of made sense. Finally, I glanced at him. "Why didn't you ask for my help sooner?"

Alexander didn't answer, but I could sense his response–he hadn't wanted to ask me for help.

Bottles, shattered glass, pieces of metal, wire, and other unpleasant things littered the ground. I tried to walk quietly. Alexander seemed to know where he was going, though he looked about constantly, alert. I followed his example, senses stretched out.

The "don't look here" feel was present but weak, as if it were left over, the caster no longer present. Or perhaps he conserved his powers. I wasn't sure.

I glanced at Alexander. He shrugged. I was grateful he was so reassuring.

We threaded our way through crates, pallets, and abandoned refuse of a more productive time. Here and there, even in this cold, I could hear the scurry of a rat, but the air remained still and quiet. Almost too quiet. Alexander's breathing and the thudding of his heart were the loudest sounds. Now and again, I caught an unpleasant whiff of something I tried to ignore. I suspected it would have been a lot worse if it hadn't been cold out.

The "don't look here" feeling felt slightly stronger to my left, and I angled that way, twisting through a maze of old pallets. Now that I knew what I was looking for, it didn't have nearly the affect it had the day before.

Alexander followed. His nervousness rose, tasting delicious. Though I wasn't hungry, my ever-present desire for blood spiked, and I had to fight to focus.

"Meg?" Alexander whispered, standing close.

His proximity did not help my control.

"Sorry." My tone harsh.

"Are you okay?"

"No." I drew out the word, hoping he would back off.

"Okay." He nodded, seeming to understand.

I pointed toward the strongest concentration of glamour, and he brushed past me. He touched my bare arm and snapped my control. I shoved him against a stack of pallets, my body pressed against his, trapping him, teeth on his neck, hand tangled in his hair as I wrenched his head backward, all before I even registered that I had moved.

"Megan!" His voice came out strangled through the awkward angle of his throat.

I gasped, trying to regain control, body shaking with need, desire, and fear. I finally wrenched myself away from him, falling to my knees on the rubble-strewn ground, gasping, trying not to cry in horror of what I'd almost done.

"Meg," Alexander said softly.

"What?" I managed to say. I had expected anger, not concern.

"It's not your fault. I think it's the glamour. He knows a vampire is after him now. I shouldn't have touched you."

I shook. "I don't know if I can fight it." I sounded weak, afraid. I didn't like it at all.

"You can. I can help shield you as well, now that we know."

I wasn't sure I believed him, wasn't sure it wasn't my own lack of control that caused the problem. I knew what his blood tasted like, and it was good. I couldn't deny I wanted more. I also couldn't help but notice how nice it had felt, pressed up against him, my teeth on his neck. I groaned and buried my face in my hands, pulling my attention away from impure thoughts about my best friend's boyfriend. Damn it. I hoped he couldn't tell what I was thinking about.

"If you need to leave, I can go alone." The arrogance was back.

I wasn't sure if he did it on purpose, but it pissed me off enough to regain control of myself. I growled at him.

Alexander put his hands in front of him, but smirked at me.

"Right. I'm going to let a Faerie boy go off by himself to get killed."

Alexander clenched his jaw. "Then you'd better get off the ground, because the night is wasting."

I bared my fangs at him and felt slightly gratified to see him flinch before I climbed to my feet. We walked further into the pallet labyrinth, finally reaching its end.

"I think he's there." I pointed. "Or at least, he was there." I hoped he wasn't there now.

Alexander nodded, studying the metal shack that butted up against the side of the old warehouse. Probably intended as a storage shed, it had flat metal sheets tacked haphazardly to a wooden frame.

"Can you tell if anyone is inside?"

I focused on the shed and shrugged.

"You should be able to sense them. I think vampires can see into the infrared."

"Really? That's kind of cool. How?"

"I'm not a vampire if you hadn't noticed. I have no idea."

I sighed and stared at the shed again, trying to see heat. After a minute of concentration, my vision shifted, startling me. I looked around wildly. Alexander blazed in my vision, warm, red, tasty. I wrenched my gaze away from him and looked around.

Everything was cold, and it was hard to distinguish buildings from ground, though there were differences. I saw a slight warmth in the shed, and I took a step forward before I could stop myself. Something told me it wasn't what we were after.

"Something is in there," I said after a minute. "I don't know what, though."

"Okay."

I frowned, trying to fix my vision, and after a short time, it shifted back to normal. I blinked a few times, trying to adjust.

"That was weird."

Alexander nodded. "I don't suggest doing that in public. Your eyes get all black."

I nodded but didn't respond, approaching the storage shed slowly with Alexander close behind me. It was quiet around the shed. A deeper quiet than before. We seemed to cross a threshold and the "don't look here" feeling faded completely, startling in its absence. I traded a look with Alexander before carefully placing my hand on the door. I didn't die, and nothing seemed to happen, so I gripped the handle and turned. The handle resisted, and I jerked it hard. Something snapped inside the knob, and it turned freely, but the bolt still resisted.

"You broke it."

"No shit." Angry, I yanked the door open. Wood cracked and splintered as the deadbolt pulled out of the doorframe, splitting the silence.

Alexander rolled his eyes before stepping around me into the dark shed. He murmured something under his breath, and a warm glow gradually surrounded his head.

I snickered as the Tinker Bell analogy came back. I could sense Alexander's annoyance, but he gave no visible indication that he'd heard. He kneeled on the floor. I glanced behind us one more time before focusing on the body on the ground.

She was dark-haired, plump, and very unconscious. I couldn't smell blood, or rather, I could smell the blood sluggishly flowing through her veins, but none of it had been spilled. Her chest rose and fell slowly as if she slept deeply.

Alexander touched her hesitantly, brushing the hair out of her face.

"You have noticed that all of his recent victims bear a striking resemblance to Ann, haven't you?" I turned to scan the empty yard again. I knew he had, but I had to say it.

Alexander took a deep breath, and his anger surged. It wasn't directed at me though, and he didn't answer. I could feel the answer in the tension in the air, and the fear that colored his thoughts. Maybe he really did like Ann.

"Just making sure."

Alexander looked up at me, the anger in his blue eyes making me flinch.

"You do know that he was choosing your victims to kill, don't you?" he said, voice harsh.

"I had noticed that actually and wondered why."

"It makes them taste better, and finding fresh vampire victims is difficult. Your kind, fortunately, aren't real common. He'll hunt your victims for a while, then eventually, he'll hunt you and move on to a new city."

"So, those missing vampires Tad found were real?"

"I'm sure some of them were. Probably not all of them."

"Excellent," I said sarcastically. "We should get her out of here."

Alexander nodded. I turned, looking out in the yard again. Something moved through the shadows of the building directly across from us, and I took a step forward, trying to see what it was. I willed my vision to change and looked again. A small blotch of red crouched by a pallet. I thought it might be a dog and listened, catching the faint beating of a heart.

I made my vision return to normal, easier the second time around, and glanced at Alexander. He stared at me, eyes filled with concern.

"Saw something. I think it's just a dog."

Alexander stared out into the night before nodding. "Okay. Do you mind carrying her? You're stronger than I am."

For a minute I thought about making a smart ass remark, but I was a vampire and that meant, girl or not, I probably was stronger.

"Sure." I knelt by the prone girl and studied her for a minute. I'd never carried a person before and wasn't quite sure how to go about picking her up. Finally, I grabbed her arm and pulled her forward until I pulled her into a sitting position. Then, I slid my arms under her legs and supported her back, grunting with the effort of dead-lifting her from the ground.

She was surprisingly light. Somehow, I'd expected her to be heavy, despite my strength. She was a little awkward to hold, but otherwise, I'd be fine.

"Let's get out of here," Alexander whispered. The golden light faded from the halo around his head.

I nodded. "It seems like we're being watched." A heavy feeling settled on me.

"Yes." Alexander drew a knife from his jacket and held it, still sheathed, in front of him.

"Umm, you have to take the sheath off."

He gave me a dirty look. "It's cold iron. I can't touch it. A full Sidhe couldn't even carry it. I'll ditch the sheath if I need to."

We made it into the maze of pallets before the air around us turned frigid, cooling so fast even my breath fogged.

Alexander cursed, unsheathing his blade. It gleamed wickedly in the low light. He held it firmly, but well away from his body, obviously uncomfortable with it.

I shivered, fear making my limbs feel weak and my insides watery. Something laughed, a sound more felt than heard, echoing through my body. I turned, trying to locate the source, but it seemed to come from everywhere.

"We should run," I said after a minute.

"You run. Get her out of here. I can't keep up with you."

I considered it, shame warming my cheeks as I did so.

"No."

The voice laughed again, and I thought I heard "good" hiss through the air, the word curling around me, making my spine tingle.

"No, really. You should get out of here. I'll be fine."

"I can still read your thoughts, Alexander."

I bent, putting the girl on the ground and stood. Cold hands closed around my arms, fingers crushing muscle to bone. I cried out as teeth tore into my shoulder. Rage enveloped me, and I thrashed, immobilized, unable to see my attacker.

The thing holding me screamed in pain and flung me into the air. I crashed into one of the stacks of pallets. They splintered around me, digging into my back, piercing my arm and scraping my bare skin. I felt a momentary surge of panic, but nothing pierced my heart, and though I didn't know if that legend was correct or not, I didn't want to find out the hard way.

Blood soaked my shirt while I lay there. Pain ripped through me when I shifted my body. I tried not to move, hoping Alexander would be able to help me, hoping the cold iron knife would scare off the evil Faerie, and we could go home safe and sound.

Alexander cried out in pain, dispelling my fantasy. Not stopping to think about what I did, I flung myself off the pallets, ignoring the pain as the wood tore at my skin. I leapt across the stacks of wood, amazed at how far the Unseelie had thrown me and at how far I could jump. Distantly, I wondered if I could fly.

I paused, crouching. A figure, cloaked in shadow and hard to focus on, had Alexander in an arm lock. It seemed to be kneeling on Alexander's back and hissed at him in a language I didn't understand. The hot scent of Alexander's spicy blood filled the air with a heady flavor.

I scanned the ground, franticly searching for the cold iron dagger. I spotted the hilt, standing out against the trampled snow, blade buried out of sight. I flung myself at it, heedless of being seen. I had to get to it.

The creature screamed in a language I didn't understand. Something heavy slammed into my back just as my fingers closed around the heavy hilt. Hot fire ripped through my back. I think I screamed as I turned over, thrusting the dagger out in front of me. The crushing weight lifted, the creature snarling as it backed away. I held the knife clutched in my hands, trembling as the excessive coldness lifted, and the oppressive feel to the night faded away. My breaths came in gasps, and though I didn't need to breathe, the remembered response was strong, and I fought to breathe normally before I hyperventilated.

"Megan?" Alexander gasped.

I could feel his pain, filtered through the haze of my own. I rolled over and forced myself to stand, tucking the dagger in my belt, not caring if I cut myself. I staggered over to Alexander and fell to my knees, ignoring the tearing muscles in my back. He bled heavily, and I forced myself to ignore the intoxicating scent.

"Are you okay?"

"Sure. Help me up."

Alexander groaned when I got him in a sitting position, and the smell of blood grew stronger. His skin was more pale than normal, and he was sweating by the time I had him upright. Blood oozed from the jagged tears in his side, which I suspected looked like my back did. I ripped his shirt the rest of the way off of him and tied it tightly around his waist. Ignoring the smell of his blood grew harder, but I managed, mostly because I was very afraid.

"The girl," he said through gritted teeth.

I glanced over where I had left her, but I could already smell her blood seeping into the ground, leaking from her torn throat.

"He killed her."

Alexander swore.

"Come on. Let's get you home." I put his arm around my shoulder and ignored the excruciating pain as I staggered away from the dead girl. I needed help, and I wasn't sure who to call. In a different situation I would have called my brother, but he wouldn't understand at all. Gary...maybe he could help. But I didn't have his number.

"Do you have your phone?"

"What?"

I could feel Alexander's attention wavering, fighting unconsciousness.

"Cell phone?"

"Yeah." He fell silent, but I caught a picture in his thoughts of his phone in his back pants pocket.

I hesitated for a moment, but the situation was dire, and I didn't think he'd even remember me pulling something out of his pocket. I stopped long enough to dial Steph's number and hoped I didn't wake everyone up. I didn't have time for a text message.

"Who is this?" Steph's groggy voice was very welcome, despite the anger and confusion I could hear.

"It's Meg. This is Alexander's phone. I need you to call Gary and see if he knows first aid. If he does, get him to meet me at Alexander's house."

"Are you okay?"

"Yeah. Alexander isn't. Look I need to get him home. Call Gary. I have to go."

"Okay. Call me when you get there. I want to know what happened."

"Yeah. I will." I started to feel faint, too, the world going black at the edges of my vision. I had a feeling we'd never wake up if we passed out outside the safety of Alexander's house. I shoved his phone into my pocket, ignoring the blood I smeared on it, mine and Alexander's mixing in an intoxicating way.

I had to stop several times on the way to his house and get away from him. I wanted Alexander's blood so badly, and he was bleeding all over me, getting away was the only way I could keep a handle on myself.

I breathed a sigh of relief when I reached the woods surrounding his house. That breath almost became a fatal mistake–for Alexander. Shoving him against a tree, I scrambled away. I sank my teeth into my own wrist to appease my blood hunger, even though I had his blood on me, too. I knew if I tasted any of his, I would lose the small control I had left. Drinking a little of my own blood cleared the memory of the taste of Fae blood temporarily. Shuddering with need, I retrieved Alexander and we stumbled the rest of the way to his home.

Gary, Tad, and Gage were waiting for me. One of them caught Alexander, and I felt warm hands grasp me as I collapsed.

"What the hell happened?"

"We need to get inside. Check Alexander's pockets." The world faded to black.

Chapter 20

The words I woke to almost sent me into a panic.

"She needs a hospital," Gary said.

"No," I heard a quieter voice reply, maybe over a phone.

"No," I echoed, appalled at the weakness in my voice.

"Megan, you're hurt bad."

"Tell me something I don't know." I groaned, trying to ignore the taste of blood that hung heavy on the air, trying to ignore the warm, beating hearts pulsing human blood through thin veins that stood so close. I again lay on Alexander's island counter. I could sense him, awake in the next room–in pain, but alive.

"Steph asked me not to call for an ambulance, but something tore you up. You need stitches."

"Alexander needs stitches." I gritted my teeth as I sat up. The world spun, and Gary held my shoulders so I wouldn't fall. I managed not to tackle him to the floor for his blood, mostly because I didn't have the energy to fight him for it just yet.

"Gage knows basic first aid, including stitches. He's taking care of Alexander since he refused to go to the hospital, too. What happened?"

"We were hunting," I gasped out. My voice sounded stronger, but only a little. "We found the thing killing the girls. It wasn't real friendly." I tried to take a few steps, not really knowing where I wanted to go, when my legs gave out again. Some uber-powerful vampire I was.

Gary caught me, picking me up before I could react. I clamped my mouth shut and forced myself to not breathe. I was so close to his neck I could almost taste his blood.

He carried me into the living room where Gage was finishing up with Alexander.

"Will you sit down now?" Gary asked, irritated.

Tad watched the proceedings with quiet curiosity and handing Gage things when he asked for them.

Alexander met my eyes. "Are you okay?"

"No." I emphasized the word as I had earlier in the pallet maze, and Alexander actually laughed.

I smiled back and stayed on the couch where Gary set me. I really didn't want to know how bad the damage was, but I thought I could feel splinters of wood sliding around in my skin.

"Why would you take Meg hunting with you?" Gary practically growled at Alexander.

The mirth faded from his eyes, and he looked down at his hands. The stitches looked nasty and numerous. I had no idea how he'd been able to sit through it. Gage rubbed some of the pungent salve on Alexander's side.

I could feel the dull ache of his injuries go numb through our mental connection as the salve absorbed into his system, and wished it worked that well for me.

"And why the hell won't either of you go to the hospital?" Gage sounded angry. And afraid.

"And what did you find?" Tad asked quietly.

I traded another look with Alexander before staring at the ground. I had no idea what to say.

"Meg is special," Alexander said after a long pause. "I believe her abilities are what led Steph to come up with her ill-advised idea to solve supernatural crime in the first place."

I nodded, still staring at the floor.

"I..." He hesitated again. "I have some ability in that direction, as well, and my, um, family has tasked me with tracking down this killer."

"'Some ability?' What does that mean?" Gage sounded suspicious.

Alexander glared at Gage. "It means that Megan and I are probably the best hope of stopping this thing. Unfortunately, it is very powerful, and I'm not. Megan is. She just doesn't know it yet."

I looked up, the sudden movement graying out my vision again.

"At the very least, you have the strongest self-control I've ever seen." He sounded surprised.

I sighed, but had no good answer.

"So what, you're some kind of Fae like Megan said?" Gage finally asked. Alexander's eyes went wide, and he looked at me.

"Uh." My eloquence failed me, so I let him see the memory through our fading link.

"I see." He shook his head. "You really are a pain in the ass."

"I do my best. Oh. Here's your knife." I smiled wickedly, removing it from my belt and sliding across the coffee table to him.

Alexander gave me a dirty look, but didn't pick it up.

"Well," Gary finally said. "I think we deserve some answers." Alexander looked at me again. I shrugged.

"I'm half Sidhe." Alexander sounded resigned. "My mother is human."

The guys absorbed that knowledge in silence.

I could feel my back healing already, not like the wound from the enchanted knife, which was still present, a thin white scar on my forearm. The lightheadedness faded quickly, though I could still feel my back muscles pull funnily when I moved. The hunger was returning with a passion, demanding to be fed like a living thing. The smell of Alexander's blood was not helping.

"Okay. So what is Meg?" Gage looked like he wanted the shotgun he styled himself after.

I squirmed, stood, glanced out the window, and went into the kitchen. I caught a mental suggestion of a dark green wine bottle in the back of his fridge and decided to ignore my annoyance at being used to fetch for a faerie. My fingers tingled as I grasped the neck of the bottle, and I grumbled as I went back into the living room.

"Anything else," I snarled.

"Thank you, Meg." Alexander's voice still lacked the usual arrogance. I knew he thanked me for more than the bottle.

"We're even now. I saved your life. You saved mine."

Alexander arched his eyebrows but nodded, uncorking the bottle.

"You really don't need to be drinking alcohol right now," Gage said darkly.

Alexander took a long drink before shaking his head. "It's not alcohol."

My nose had already told me that, but I was surprised to hear him admit it.

"It is a kind of medicine for Sidhe."

I giggled. "Tinker Bell medicine." Okay, so I still felt a little light-headed. His flash of irritation made me giggle harder. "Ow. Stop making me laugh. It still hurts." My muscles protested the abuse, cramping. I had to sink to the ground, still snorting at the mental image I had conjured.

"I am not making you laugh."

"Right. So, you didn't answer my question–what is Meg?" Gary said again.

"I'm complicated. Leave it alone." I added power to my voice, not at all interested in answering his question.

They immediately dropped it.

"It's getting late. I have to get home." The sky outside began to lighten, and I needed food.

Alexander must have been aware of my hunger. He looked at the green container he held, and then glanced at me. "I don't know if it will help, but you can try some of this." He held out the bottle hesitantly.

I took it and sniffed. It didn't smell repellant, so, conscious of the four pairs of eyes watching me, I took a hesitant sip. I don't know what I was expecting, but nothing awful happened. Instead, warmth radiated out from my stomach.

"Huh." I drank more, a slightly larger cautious mouthful. It seemed to help. The hunger subsided. I actually felt better than I had in months, except maybe when I'd tasted Alexander's blood. I took one more mouthful before handing it back. "I do feel better. Thank you."

I also guessed by the uneasy feeling I could sense from him that he wasn't supposed to share the contents of the wine bottle with me. Oh well, what was done was done, and I no longer felt the urge to jump Gary for his blood.

"Thanks."

He nodded.

I stood and went over to the window, the day now considerably lighter than it had been before. I stared at the sky, horrified at the bright, baby-blue showing through the colorful sunrise. Of all the days for it to be sunny.

"Shit." I stepped away from the window as the sun rose enough to cast rays of warmth through the glass panes. My skin tingled, and I backed away, belatedly thinking I should have shut it.

"What's wrong?" Tad asked when I brushed against him, still moving away from the window.

"Gary, could you shut the curtains please?" Alexander sounded resigned.

A wave of weariness flooded through my veins, turning my limbs to lead weights. I just wanted to curl up someplace dark and sleep. I sat when I bumped into a chair. I kept staring at the now-curtained window, fear blanking out rational thought. I was trapped, away from home–not safe. The litany kept running through my head, preventing me from answering Tad's question. Not that I wanted to.

"Megan, it's okay. You can stay here for the day. I have rooms without windows. Hell, I have a basement. Calm down."

I continued to stare, not really comprehending what he said.

Vampire bitch, he snarled into my head.

I jumped and turned toward him, a return snarl on my lips. His words sounded as loud in my head as if he had spoken them. I wasn't entirely sure he hadn't, but the mild look on his face and the confused ones on the guy's faces let me know he hadn't spoken aloud.

"What?"

"You can stay here for the day. Relax."

"Don't frigging tell me to relax, Faerie boy. My mom is home, and so is my brother. They are going to notice I'm gone. And while normally they might not freak out, with all the murders, they're gonna call the cops. So no, I can't just go home tonight and convince them I'm fine, because by then, it will be too frigging late."

His unspoken thought echoed in my mind as if it were my own. *Have you ever considered that it might be better if you didn't go home?* It shot through my head like a virus, eating away at a little more of my resolve to try and live a normal life. I had thought it before, but hearing it from him, even if he hadn't actually said it, made it more real.

I growled. Alexander held his hands up, trying to be calming. I kept glaring.

"Fine. I'll take care of it. You did say you'd only help me if you were home in time, and I prevented that, so I should fix it."

I opened my mouth to protest. I did not want to owe him anything.

"No. As I said, it's my fault." He twisted to look at Gage. "Can you give me a ride?"

Gage traded a glance with Tad and Gary before nodding warily.

"Wait. What are you going to do?"

Alexander grinned. "Haven't you ever heard of changelings?"

I gaped at him, not quite comprehending what he meant, but before I could react, he left the house.

"Oh, God." Was he really going to pretend to be me?

I sank back into the chair, exhaustion momentarily forgotten as I contemplated Alexander pretending to be me in my house. I hoped he was smart enough to get Mom to let me call in sick, instead of trying to go to my classes.

"Okay. So what the hell was that all about?" Gary glared at me.

I could sense a glimmer of anger from him, and I felt bad.

"Um. I'm allergic to direct sunlight. It's a..." I trailed off as Gary blanched, and Tad sat up, staring at me. The tension in the room spiked, and I silently cursed.

Admitting my sunlight allergy was as good as admitting I was a vampire. I blamed it on the sunrise. It made me sluggish, and I was having a hard time staying awake, let alone carrying on a delicate conversation.

"I've seen you outside during the day," Tad finally said, slowly.

I shut my eyes, trying to think. "It's a side effect of my supernatural abilities." Well, that much was true. "Direct sunlight is very uncomfortable."

"'Very uncomfortable' and 'I can't go home' are two different things." Gary kept eye contact with me, though I wanted to look away.

I felt like crying. I couldn't think of a way out of the hole I'd dug, and I was just so tired.

"Why does it matter?"

"We dropped everything we were doing this morning to help you out. I think we deserve some answers." Gary's brown eyes flashed in anger, and his normally pleasant expression was dark.

Anger surged through me, and I stood before I gave conscious thought to what I was doing.

"Fine, maybe you do deserve answers," I growled, meeting his glare with my own. "But are you sure you really want them?"

Gary took a step away from me, and I could feel–almost see–Tad move with my strange ability to sense everything around me. His fingers closed around the dagger I had left on the coffee table earlier.

I shoved Gary into the wall before he could react, my face inches from his. He was taller, but I had him off balance. If I let go of the shirt I had clutched in my fist, he would probably fall. "Really, do you want them?"

Gary's fear saturated the air, filling me like a fine wine. I took a deep breath, inhaling the intoxicating fear scent, still locking eyes with him. I let him see the hunger his fear aroused in my eyes. He blanched.

Tad stood behind me now, holding the dagger, but I could sense his uncertainty, too.

"Go ahead, Tad. Stab me. Really piss me off." Tad backed away, setting the knife down. I could feel the tension in Gary's muscles, the shortness of his breath, the pounding of his heart. It was difficult to let him go, but I did, stepping back, still keeping eye contact.

Finally, Gary nodded, eyes wide and expression serious. "I do want to know."

I bared my fangs at him and almost laughed when he stumbled away from me, backing against the wall I'd had him shoved into.

"Shit."

"It's inconvenient," I muttered, turning away.

"What?" Tad stepped away when I glanced at him.

I didn't show him my teeth, though. Once was hard enough.

"She's a vampire." Fear made Gary's voice break.

Tad paled and glanced at the dagger on the table, as if regretting putting it down.

I shook my head. "It won't do you a lot of good." I sank down into one of the armchairs and buried my face in my hands, fighting tears. My back still ached, and I'd failed to save the girl's life, and now, Gary and Tad knew what I was, and it was all too much.

I didn't realize I was shaking until Tad put his hand on my shoulder. I froze, not knowing what to expect, but he left his hand there and knelt next to me.

"How long?" His voice was soft.

I looked up, fortunately dry-eyed. "Couple of months."

"Steph and Ann know?"

I snorted. "That's why Steph started this little club in the first place. Because of what happened to me."

"You can go outside during the day?" Tad's voice turned inward as if he was cataloging everything, but his hand remained on my shoulder, warm and comforting.

"Yeah, just not in direct sunlight. Alexander doesn't know why."

"Well." Gary cleared his throat. "I guess that explains a lot." He laughed, though it sounded strained. "Like how you can get into bars."

I shut my eyes. "Yeah." Tad and Gary exchanged glances, and I could imagine their disgust. I shivered, wondering what they were going to do. I expected fear or hatred.

I wasn't prepared when Tad sat down on the edge of the chair and put his arms around me. Surprised, I didn't resist when he pulled me into his arms and held me.

I started to cry.

Chapter 21

Tad held me while I cried. I didn't sniffle, as my nose stayed clear. I just shook, red tears leaking from my tightly shut eyes. I kept my face hidden, buried against Tad's lean chest. The position was awkward, pulling at my healing back, but I didn't care.

I finally managed to stop crying, embarrassed at my outburst, but I didn't pull away. I hadn't realized how much I'd wanted someone to hold me, and while Tad wasn't telling me it would be all right, his presence was good enough.

Though I did wonder why he bothered. I hadn't said more than a handful of words to him, and most of those had barely been civil.

"I'm sorry," I finally said. "It's been a long night."

Tad laughed, but didn't let go, and I didn't move.

"It's okay. I imagine you're tired. You should get some sleep."

I nodded, his words like a magic spell. My eyelids drooped, and I yawned.

"I should get cleaned up first. I'm covered in blood," I managed to say through my yawns. My bloody tears dampened Tad's dark shirt, but it wasn't obvious, except to my nose, and some of the blood covering me covered him, too. He didn't seem concerned about it.

"Yes, you are."

Tad helped me stand, and then suddenly conscious of how close I stood to him, I backed away, rubbing at my damp face.

"Sorry." I could feel myself blushing.

"It's okay, Meg. I just wouldn't tell Gage."

I looked up, meeting his eyes. "Sure. I'd rather you didn't tell anyone."

"We won't," Gary said from across the room.

I could see the questions in his eyes, but I didn't have the energy to deal with them anymore. I turned and fled the room, finding my way upstairs and into a room that didn't feel like it was used much. An attached bathroom drew my attention, and I stripped off my shredded clothing and looked in the mirror, twisting so I could see my back. It was a mess. A healing mess, but still pretty torn up. There were a few spots, places that looked like puncture wounds, that weren't healing, but right then, I was too tired to care. I ignored the pain of the hot water, grateful to be clean, and dried off, leaving red smears on the towel. Then, I crawled into bed naked and hoped I didn't bleed on the clean white sheets, but quickly, I was beyond caring as I gave myself to sleep.

I woke after dark, feeling rested, though I was sore. My abused and torn muscles twitched when I crawled out of bed, but I ignored them. I looked around the room cautiously, aware something had changed while I slept. A pile of clothing lay on the end of my bed, and the thought that someone had been in here while I was unconscious made me shiver. I touched the clothes, able to smell Alexander's scent on them, spicy blood combined with something I couldn't quite identify other than that it belonged to him. He hadn't brought me underwear, and though a fresh set would have been nice, I didn't like picturing Alexander digging through my underwear drawer.

My old pair was soaked in blood, but my bra had somehow survived mostly intact, so I put it back on and pulled my pants over bare skin. It felt weird, but I'd survive. I gathered my ruined clothes and let myself out of the bedroom.

It was dark in the hallway, but I could hear voices downstairs. Alexander had come back, Tad, Gage, and Gary were there, and so were Steph and Ann. I was so glad Steph and Ann had come, I wanted to run downstairs, but the pain in my back from the wounds that weren't healing kept me at a walk.

Alexander was the first to notice me lurking in the doorway, and he gestured imperiously for me to join them.

I glared at him before walking stiffly into the room.

"Meg!" Steph jumped up from where she'd been sitting next to Gary and hugged me tightly. Ann stood, greeting me a little more sedately, but she still seemed relieved to see me.

"We were so worried. Alexander told us what happened." Ann blushed when Steph mentioned her boyfriend.

I sighed. "Sorry." I glanced quickly at Tad and Gary before looking away, not wanting to meet their eyes. Gage I tried to ignore, but I could tell by the way he looked at me, eyes boring holes in my back, that he knew something was up.

I caught a quick confirmation from Alexander through our fading mental connection that Gary and Tad had changed their minds and told Gage what I was.

Damn.

"Are you feeling any better?" Tad finally asked when the silence threatened to become awkward.

"Some. I think I have chunks of wood in my back still."

"We need to get those out."

I nodded, not looking forward to that. Alexander looked over at Gage.

"Oh, hell, no. Vampire girl can help herself." He glared at me.

That was too much. Anger flared through me, and I met his eyes, challenging him with my posture.

"Look, asshole. I didn't ask for this, and trust me, if I could give it back, I would. And you're just going to have to fucking deal with it."

He tilted his head, not breaking the silence that followed my outburst. Then, he smiled broadly. "Cool."

I frowned, but all sense of anger from him was gone. I snapped my jaw shut and shook my head. I did not understand the male half of the species at all.

I saw Gary shake his head out of the corner of my eye and decided the drama was probably over for now. I contemplated sitting in one of the chairs, but decided it would hurt worse than standing, so I tried to make myself comfortable while everyone sat and stared at each other. It was almost laughable.

"Come on." Gage stood. "Let's get you taken care of."

I arched an eyebrow at him.

"I'm apparently the resident first-aid guy. I'll get the wood out of your back."

"Okay. Thanks." I walked into the kitchen, and, of course, everyone followed.

"Want me to lie on the island?"

"Yeah."

And yet again, I found myself lying on Alexander's counter. Though this time, I lay on my stomach with a pillow under my chest so I could be a little more comfortable, with my shirt hitched up around my shoulders. It would have been just as easy to take it off, but I couldn't quite bring myself to take my shirt off in front of everybody.

Gage whistled when he saw my back. "Tore you up good."

"Yeah. You should have seen it yesterday." I gritted my teeth when he touched my back, prodding at the wounds that refused to heal.

"This is probably going to hurt," he warned.

"Gee, you think? Just do it." I managed to stay quiet for most of it, but the last piece Gage drew out was a particularly long shard. I whimpered, lips clamped shut to prevent the louder cry that tried to work its way out of my mouth.

"Sorry, dude." Gage sounded distracted with concentration.

"It's fine," I managed to say through my clenched jaw.

"Damn, someone with bad aim try to stake you or something?"

"No, our bad guy threw me at high velocity into a pile of wood."

"Ah."

I lay there once he finished, willing the pain to fade. It didn't seem to help, so I finally rolled over, trying to preserve some semblance of modesty.

"Thank you," I said once I had my shirt pulled back down.

"Sure."

"We should probably get going." I looked at the clock on the stove. It was almost eight. I glanced at Alexander.

"You'll want to go in through your window, but they won't have thought about you all day."

"Thanks."

He nodded and turned to Steph and Ann. "Don't go anywhere outside of home or school without Meg."

Ann asked, "Why not?"

"Because she might be able to protect you."

"Okay. How are we getting home?" I looked at the guys.

"We'll give you a ride. Come on."

"Umm...your truck isn't big enough for all of us."

Gage grinned. "It'll be cozy. Come on."

Gage's pickup had one of those tiny back seats that was really only good for dogs or groceries, but Ann, Steph, and

Gary squeezed into it. Gage drove, of course, and I got to sit bitch between him and Tad. Oh, and Gage's truck was a stick. I sat pressed up against Tad so Gage wasn't reaching between my legs to shift gears.

Tad finally put his arm on the back of the seat, and while it was much more comfortable, it was also a lot more awkward, especially after last night. I stared at the dash while the truck lurched and bumped down the road and tried not to lean against him too much.

"Damn, Gage, your truck rides rougher than Meg's Jeep. I wasn't sure that was possible." Steph laughed after a while.

Gage grinned. "Real trucks ride rough."

I snorted, but didn't bother to contradict him. He was right.

I did my best to project an aura of "I'm not here" while we dropped Ann and Steph off. Tad climbed in the back after we let Steph out at her place, and I felt disappointed, missing his warmth pressed up against me.

Of course, he was probably relieved he didn't have to be so close to me now.

"Drop me off here," I said when we got to the corner of my street. "I don't want anyone seeing the truck. I have to sneak in."

"Sure."

Gage pulled over. I put my hand on the door handle, but his touch on my shoulder stopped me.

"I have to ask."

I met his eyes. "What?" I was pretty sure I didn't want to hear his question.

"How many people have you killed?"

I hadn't been expecting that. "Um...recently or over my whole life?"

Gage frowned. "I'm serious. I didn't want to ask in front of your friends." Implying, of course, that he wasn't my friend.

I sighed. "I haven't killed anyone, Gage."

"You're sure?"

"Completely. I have not so much as killed a fly in months, though once the flies come back, they will learn to fear my super-fast reflexes." I smiled.

"How is that possible?"

I shrugged. "Alexander said I had amazing self-control. Maybe that's why. I don't know. I don't want to kill anyone, but if this Unseelie comes after me or any of you, I'm going to make sure he's dead."

Gage nodded. "Good. Keep it that way."

"Doing my best. Can I go now?"

"Sure."

"See y'all later." I made it inside with a minimum of effort, and no one bothered me that night, though I could smell Alexander's spicy scent in my room. He'd slept in my bed, which was more than a little disconcerting.

It was overcast the next morning and I managed to force myself out of bed, though I still felt exhausted. Fortunately, the wounds on my back had all closed, and while they still felt tender, it wouldn't bother me so much.

John tried to catch my attention before I left, but I ran out the door, pretending not to hear. I didn't want to talk to him just then, and I didn't want to be late to school. I was running behind. I made it right before the first bell rang and only had time to throw things in my locker before running to my first class. Classes seemed to stretch on into eternity. I couldn't concentrate. I was tired enough and bored enough that they seemed pointless, though several of my classes were going over what would be on the semester term tests. I tried to care, but it just didn't seem very important.

The bell for lunch brought some relief, and I met Steph in our normal corner. We chatted for a while, but Ann didn't show.

"Where's Ann?"

"I don't know. Maybe she's with Jennifer and Candice?" Steph shrugged.

"Maybe. We should find out."

"Why?"

"She could be in trouble. That Unseelie thing was targeting people who looked like her, if you hadn't noticed. I think it was a warning to Alexander to back off. What if that thing decided the warning wasn't enough?"

Steph shrugged. "I'm sure she's fine, but we can go look."

We scanned the lunch area, but they weren't there, so we went to the cafeteria. The hint of lavender that seemed to hover around Candice was stronger, and I followed it around a couple of locker banks to a corner where Candice and Jennifer were lounging on the floor, eating their lunches. Both looked worried, but it didn't stop them from sneering when they saw us.

"Have you seen Ann?"

"What, did she get tired of hanging out with you?" Candice sneered.

"No. I haven't seen her today, and I'm worried. Have. You. Seen. Her?" I lent the words a touch of power.

Candice frowned. "No. We haven't seen her."

I traded a look with Steph and dug out my phone. I hit the speed dial for Ann's phone, and it rang several times before the voice mail picked up.

"Damn it." I looked through my recent call log for Alexander's number. "Try Ann again." I walked away from Candice and Jennifer.

Steph tried Ann's phone again while I listened to Alexander's ring. Finally, it picked up.

"Hello," I said when the line stayed quiet.

A voice hissed, "Ahh, the vampire.... Looking for your friends? Heh, you won't see them again. Black hair is tasty, and Strawberry is next." The creature laughed. "And then a final treat. I do like vampire."

"When I find you," I growled into the phone, "I am going to rip your throat out and drain the life from your veins."

The creature on the other end of the phone laughed. The line went dead.

I glared at the phone.

"Meg?" Steph's voice shook.

Several other students were looking at me, confusion and a touch of fear on their faces. Candice and Jennifer were standing close enough to hear.

"It has both of them. I have to go."

"Meg, go where? Do you even know where they are?"

"I have an idea." I thrust my backpack at Steph. "The keys to the Jeep are in there. Take it home tonight. Go straight home. It wants you, too. Stay safe."

"Meg, wait. You need help."

I was already running for the door.

Chapter 22

Normally, I would have been freaking out, wondering how I would find the Unseelie and my friends, but by wounding me the other day, the creature had unwittingly given me the tools I needed.

Trying not to panic, I stretched out my senses, opening my mind wide, and reached for Alexander's presence. Our connection, formed from drinking his blood, though not as strong, was still there. While I couldn't tell exactly where he was, I could tell what direction I needed to go.

I ran faster.

The connection led me out of town, past the warehouses, and into the wildlife preserve. The miles of woods would be mostly deserted this time of year. There were several forest service buildings and a few abandoned cabins that a lot of us knew from semi–forbidden summer explorations when we were younger. I was willing to bet the Unseelie hid in one of those buildings.

I wasn't one of those people who knew every abandoned ruin, but I knew a few of them, and it seemed like I headed toward the half-collapsed homesteader cabin. It was one of the few with a cellar.

The forest grew quiet and still. There was no wind, and the snow deadened sound. No birds called, and even the squirrels were absent. Their absence by itself would have been enough to know something was wrong. We had a lot of squirrels.

I slowed down, not wanting to barge in completely unprepared.

"Alexander," I whispered in my mind, hoping the Unseelie couldn't somehow sense his thoughts.

He was mostly unconscious, in pain and very afraid. I pushed at his mind, willing him to wake. I could sense his eyes flutter open, feel the shock of pain as the light assaulted his sensitive eyes. His fear threatened to overwhelm me, and I clutched a tree for support.

"Meg?" He whispered my name.

I'm here. Shh... Where is Ann?

Alexander shifted his head slightly, and I could get a vague sense of her lying on the floor close to him. I could also sense the creature. He was close.

"None of that!" the creature hissed.

I doubled over as it kicked Alexander in the stomach, and I quickly broke the connection, not wanting his pain impeding me.

My phone vibrated in my pocket, startling me. I stifled a shriek and backed away from the cabin. It was a text from Steph. I quickly replied, telling her where I was, and not to follow, then I shut off my phone. I didn't want it to vibrate at the wrong moment.

"Mmm, pretty half-blood, pretty human," the creature hummed loudly, its voice discordant, not quite natural. "I know you're there, vampire. Want to join your friends?" It hissed laughter, the sound grating like nails on a chalkboard.

The voice sent chills through my body, fear making my limbs weak. What was I even doing here? I couldn't help, couldn't defeat him. I was still wounded from the last encounter we'd had. I took a step backward and almost ran.

"Meg?"

I could barely hear Ann even with my heightened senses. I couldn't leave her. Not like this. I slipped from tree to tree, trying to remain hidden, until I reached the edge of the clearing.

The creature stood by the door, looking directly at me. Shadow cloaked his figure, but he…it…whatever…would have been tall if he hadn't been stooped over. His arms were slightly too long, legs slightly too short. His features were hidden in the darkness, but I had a vivid picture in my head from the image Alexander had shared with me.

It laughed again. "I know where you are."

The creature blurred. I gasped and spun around just as it stepped from the shadow of the tree I hid next to, fingers tipped in vicious claws.

I threw myself backward, barely avoiding its grasp, even with vampire-enhanced speed.

With another laugh, it faded away. I spun around, backing away from all the trees, hoping the creature would have to show itself if I gave it no cover to jump from.

"Vampire thinks she's clever?" The creature hissed right next to me. Strong hands gripped me, claws drawing blood. "Little vampire has a shadow, too."

I screamed as I sailed through the air. Sparks exploded in my vision as my head smashed against a tree. I staggered, trying to stay upright.

"Not so clever now? I don't think you'll be taking my throat, my blood, anytime soon."

I swung at the sound of his voice, vision still blurry, and staggered when I missed. The Unseelie laughed again. "I think I'll save you for last."

Claws dug into my back. I screamed.

The world went black.

The dull ache in my head and the musty dankness in the air convinced me I was awake some time later. I lay there for a minute, not breathing, not making a sound, trying to determine if I was alone.

I thought I was. I could smell nothing but the skunky air and hear nothing that sounded like breathing or the beating of a heart. I couldn't see anything either. I forced my vision into the infrared. Vague outlines, low ceiling. I wasn't used to this kind of vision, so I couldn't identify anything, but I saw no heat. I shifted my vision back to normal, and now that I had an idea of what surrounded me, I could see a bit in the darkness.

I opened my senses as wide as I could, and a picture of the world around me formed. Even after all these months, I wasn't used to it. A broken desk sat in one corner. A sheet of ice where water had leaked in covered half the basement and wooden rafters supported a surprisingly tightly laid floor. No light filtered through the cracks. Or perhaps night had fallen. I pushed my focus outward. It was night; my veins sang with the desire to embrace the darkness. I snorted at the reaction...well, I was in the dark; I should embrace it.

Finally, I decided it should be safe to move, though I had no idea why I was alone here. I had a vague memory of the creature telling me it would be back for me.

Panic surged through me and I fought it. I had no time to panic. I had to find my friends.

The clink of metal brought my attention to something else I should have noticed earlier–heavy cuffs. Cold metal around my wrists and ankles trapped me to the ground. I did panic then, silently except for the frantic rattle of metal as I yanked hard on the confining links. I pulled until my wrists bled, the metal burning my skin.

Momentarily exhausted, I lay back on the ground, trying to think. I had no idea what to do, no tools, no ability to pick locks. I couldn't break them. Grinding my teeth together, I used my anger to fight away my tears. I reached out to Alexander. The link felt weak, so weak I couldn't tell what direction he was in, just that he was alive and in a great deal of pain.

"Well, shit," I finally said aloud.

I stared at my wrists and tugged again. It was no good; they were too tight. Though, if I could dislocate my thumb, I would be able to squeeze out of them. But I might have to break other bones, too. The wounds would heal, but it would hurt, and it wasn't going to help me get my feet free.

I'd never really studied the human hand before. It was intricate, delicate, and attached, so I would feel everything I did to it. I gritted my teeth, and before I could really think about what I was doing, I yanked–and screamed as my thumb pulled free of its socket.

One day, I would hopefully find a way to dull pain, but right now, I didn't know how. It was several minutes before I could contemplate my hand again. Still a little too tight, the cuff wouldn't quite slide off with only a dislocated thumb. Taking a deep breath, I gripped my hand and squeezed viciously, snapping tiny bones, pulping my hand.

The cuff slid free.

Sobbing in relief, I started pulling on my hand, trying to reset bones and get my thumb back in its socket. I wouldn't be able to free my other hand until this one healed, so I stared at it, willing it to heal faster. I thought it was working, but I still had to wait. I could feel every pop and snap as bones knitted and abused flesh healed. Still, it wasn't fast enough.

I was about ready to destroy my other hand, despite not being completely healed, when movement at the edge of my senses caught my attention. I stopped moving, stopped breathing, and listened. Voices, people, five of them. Familiar people. Oh, God.

I wanted to tell them to run, to yell at them to get out of here, but I needed help, so I let them come. They were quiet, speaking only a little, and they weren't close enough for me to understand what they said, so I waited.

"There it is," I heard Steph say.

They hurried forward, and I cringed, hoping the creature had left no traps, but they made it inside unmolested.

"Meg!" John called.

I hesitated, scared to see them, but I had to get out of here, had to help Ann.

"I'm down here." I blinked in the sudden, harsh light of a flashlight and looked away, willing my eyes to adjust as they had to the pitch-blackness.

"Megan!" John cried and rushed to me, wrapping me in his arms. "You idiot."

"Trust me. I am aware that I should have at least gotten Alexander's knife." I felt John's annoyance underneath his relief.

"They were here. The creature knocked me out before I could kill him. I can't break these." I held up my other hand, ignoring John's incredulous look.

Tad knelt by my side and studied the manacle. "How did you get the other one off?"

I held up my free hand. It was bruised purple in the harsh yellow light from the flashlight. "I broke it."

I could feel Tad wince. "I might be able to open these." He reached for my hand. "Let me see."

"You know how to pick locks?"

"Everybody has to have a hobby." He started on my other wrist.

Steph finally asked, "Meg, what happened?"

"I thought I told you not to follow."

"Damn lucky she did." Gage growled as he scanned the room. He had a shotgun in one hand, knives in his belt. Gary was similarly armed. Steph seemed to have at least one dagger, as did Tad. John was the only one who looked unarmed.

"Please tell me someone thought to get Alexander's knife."

Gage smiled at me and pulled one of the daggers from his belt. "Here."

"Good."

"Megan, what is going on?" John's anger and confusion were overriding his concern.

"We told you." Steph nervously scanned the basement and kept eyeing the stairs.

"Yeah, but I don't believe you."

"You will after a while." I sighed, trying not to shift impatiently while Tad worked on the chains.

"Ha!" The manacle fell open from my wrist.

"Thanks." I thrust my legs at him.

He had them off reasonably quickly, and I jumped to my feet.

"Wait. Where do you think you're going?" John grabbed at my arm as I rushed up the stairs. He missed and they followed me.

"I have to find Alexander and Ann."

"No, we need to get you to a doctor and call the police."

"I don't need a doctor. Trust me. I'm fine. A little hungry, but that's how it goes."

John looked confused. Tad took a step away from me.

"I'm fine."

"You're sure?" I knew Tad wasn't asking about my injuries.

"Uber self-control, remember?"

"Forgive me if I'm not comforted."

Brushing past John, I left the cabin, turning, trying to sense Alexander.

"Can you find them?" Steph asked after they followed me outside.

"How the hell would she be able to find them?" John grumbled.

"I can kind of sense Alexander. It's a long story."

"Seems like we have time."

I pointed. "That way."

Gage grabbed my arm, wrenching it before I could take off running. "Meg, you need our help."

"It's too dangerous."

He shoved his shotgun in my face, barrel pointed to the sky. "I have this baby loaded with cold iron shot. Loaded it myself. I think I can help."

I considered taking the gun and leaving anyway, but really, I didn't have the faintest idea of how to fire one.

"Fine. But we need to get going. I have a feeling the only reason he hasn't killed Ann yet is because he's enjoying torturing Alexander. He won't wait much longer."

"Where are we going?"

"I don't know. That way." I pointed again.

"That's back toward town." Gage thrust the keys to his truck at me. "I left my truck at the visitors' parking lot, but there is a Jeep trail over that way. I saw it on our way in. You may have to open some gates, but it will be quicker if we don't have to walk the whole way. Don't get it stuck."

I stared at him.

"Hurry."

"Right." I ran.

Chapter 23

Gage's truck was parked in a small parking lot. The engine still glowed slightly with warmth to my enhanced sight. During the run, I had accidentally figured out how to sense heat while still using normal vision. It was less confusing than only seeing heat, and a little more useful than normal vision.

I opened the door and slid behind the wheel. Gage was a lot taller than me. Fortunately, his bench seat adjusted, and I could get close enough to push the clutch to the floor. The engine roared to life, shattering the still silence of the forest. I winced, but there was no help for it, and I was sure that if the Unseelie was close enough to hear the engine, he would have already known I was there.

I didn't bother with a seatbelt and turned the truck toward the Jeep trail. The gate was shut, but a quick jerk on the cold-brittle metal fixed that. I started with the headlights on, but quickly realized I could see better without them. Seeing the variations in the ground, the ruts, the potholes, made the trip significantly easier. I spotted my friends, dark shapes glowing in the night. I turned the truck and waited for them to reach me. Gage looked like he wanted to take over, but I gestured for him to get in the back, and he didn't argue.

John stared at me as if he had no idea who I was, and, really, I couldn't blame him.

"No lights?"

"Can see better without them." I took off as soon as everyone was in, driving much faster than was really advisable, even with vampire reflexes and sight.

"I'm glad you're driving." Gage didn't sound convinced, however.

"I'm not." John sounded stressed. "Slow down."

"No time," I muttered, concentrating on the road.

We burst out of the trees into the parking lot, and I slammed on the brakes. We skidded a bit before the truck slowed enough for me to make the turn into town.

I flipped on the headlights and slammed on the gas, shifting rapidly.

"Maybe he went back to the warehouses," I wondered aloud as we sped toward town. I could have gotten there faster alone, but Gage was right. I could use the help.

"Could be," Gage said. "None of us know this part of town well. We aren't originally from here. That's why Steph called John. She couldn't remember where the cabin was, said you knew the woods better than her or Ann."

"Ah." I had wondered. It would have been better to leave him out of this. The sense I had of Alexander got stronger, and I made a quick decision to turn. The truck shuddered in my hands, and I could hear Gage whimper at the abuse.

"Sorry. It's not like I have turn-by-turn GPS."

"It's okay."

I fell silent again. We were getting close. The turn I'd taken led out to some old farmland. The fields were fallow, and the house abandoned. I'd only been there once before, so I didn't know it well.

We bounced down the long, rutted driveway that led to a two-story farmhouse with a broken-down, wraparound porch. The wood siding was falling off, paint all but gone, and there were several outbuildings that were little more than piles of weathered timber.

I could feel the moment the creature noticed us. I had been about to stop, to approach on foot, when its attention shifted, focusing on us.

I grinned. Change of plans. It didn't seem happy.

"Meg?" Tad sounded worried and a little afraid.

I stomped on the gas. "Was going to go in on foot, but really, we're surrounded by iron. It might not be cold, but have you noticed that Alexander drives a mostly plastic car?"

"Maybe he just likes newer vehicles," Steph said.

"Bet he was awfully uncomfortable when you drove him the other day." I glanced at Gage.

"Yeah, dude couldn't sit still."

"Now, if only he'll sit still long enough for me to ram him with your truck."

"What!"

"I don't think he will."

"You're not going to hit Alexander?" John said softly.

"No, but I wouldn't mind running our Unseelie friend over a time or two." I suspected the expression on my face looked feral. My hand still hurt, though it was in one piece, and he had a lot of other crimes to answer for.

"You can't just kill him," John protested.

"I intend to try."

"Megan!"

"Look, I'll explain later." *If there was a later*.

John fell silent, and I skidded the truck to a halt in front of the dark farmhouse.

"Gage, help me with this bitch," I snarled, launching myself out of the truck.

Gage followed me out, looking around. He couldn't see the darker bit of shadow I stared at.

"Aim there," I pointed, and more quickly than I would have thought, the shotgun barked, deafening me.

The creature howled, obviously not expecting the iron shot.

"You will pay for that." It hissed. Its voice surrounded us, cutting through us like ice in a storm.

"Get the others," I yelled, hoping someone would, as I charged forward, tackling the creature around its middle, the strong scent of spicy Fae blood momentarily overriding my conscious thought. I snarled, trying to bite him, all other thoughts leaving my mind.

The sharp claws digging into my ribcage filled me with rage, but cleared my mind enough for me to regain control.

I wished for my own claws as I punched at the Unseelie's face. It would have been more effective if he hadn't melted into shadow underneath me. I winced as my fist impacted the frozen ground, and rose to a crouch, spinning around, trying to locate the creature. Steph argued with Alexander inside, and John emerged with Ann in his arms.

"Get her in the truck. Alexander, get out here!" I was sure he could hear me.

He stopped arguing with Steph, and both of them ran outside.

"Now, get in the truck and get out of here." I snarled, turning, searching for the creature.

"Like hell." Gage stood close, his gun held ready in his hands.

"Meg, we need to get some place safer," Alexander yelled. "It will follow us. Get in the truck."

"Come on," Gage said.

I backed slowly to the pickup, wary of attack. "Where are we going?" I slid into the middle of the front seat. John, Steph, Gary, and Ann were crammed into the back. I ended up sitting on top of Tad and Alexander, relinquishing the driver's position to Gage.

"My place," Alexander said.

Gage nodded.

The creature's angry howl carried on the wind.

"Are you okay?" I looked at Alexander. "You're bleeding." I was angry enough at the Unseelie that the scent of Alexander's blood was only mildly distracting.

He nodded. "So are you." I could hear the strain in his voice. He was in a significant amount of pain.

"This truck is not made for this many people," Tad complained as I shifted my weight slightly.

"Sorry. I could meet you guys there."

"No. It's not safe. He can move just as fast as you can, Meg," Alexander said.

"Yeah. I know." I tried not to crush Tad and Alexander while Gage drove. "How is Ann?"

Alexander shook his head. "Unconscious, but otherwise okay. I haven't had time to try and wake her."

"Slow down. Cop!" I pointed as Gage sped around the main turn into town. Sirens lit up ahead of us.

"Shit."

Gage glanced at me. "Anything you can do about this?"

I shut my eyes. "Probably. Just slow down."

"No one move," Alexander said softly. "I'll make sure he only sees you two.

"Shift over."

I slid into the middle seat, pressed up tight against Gage. He grinned and put his arm around me. I rolled my eyes. "In your dreams," I muttered.

"Hey, sorry. Don't do fangs."

The cop sauntered up to the window, shining his flashlight into the cab. Gage rolled his window down.

"Hi, Officer."

"Do you know how fast you two were driving?"

"Forty-five," I answered, filling my voice with power.

"Forty-five," he muttered.

"I know it's a little fast." I made my voice sound sweet. "But we're running late." We'd been going closer to sixty, but the speed limit was forty, and I wasn't sure if I was good enough to completely alter his memory.

"You were going to give us a verbal warning to slow down," I suggested.

"Yes. You two get home safe now. Slow down." The officer turned, eyes a little vacant, and walked slowly back to his car.

I took a deep breath.

"What the hell was that?" John asked once the window had rolled back up.

"I'm talented." I shifted back over so Gage had room to drive, and he slowly accelerated off the shoulder.

"Faerie boy, do you have any sort of magic that can keep us from being seen?" I grinned at his flash of irritation.

"Yes. If you stop calling me that."

I snorted at his irritation. "Well, it's better than half-blood."

"Maybe." He shut his eyes.

His pain curled around me through the remnants of our mental link, and I could sense the profile of the car darken. It seemed similar to the "don't look here" magic the creature used, and I shivered as it enveloped us.

"Handy. Wish I could do that."

Alexander sighed. "You can, Megan. You can do a lot of things I can't. You just have to learn how." His voice shook.

"Got a training manual handy?"

He sighed again, but didn't reply, and I could tell the strain wore on him already. He must be hurt worse than I had thought.

I fell silent, sensing John's questions, but he kept quiet, for which I was grateful. I thought about the best way to explain this to him and felt he'd be happier if I altered his memory. Of course, I didn't know if I was good enough to do it, but I thought I would probably try. I'd deal with it later though. We made it the rest of the way without incident, though Alexander was almost unconscious by the time we arrived.

"Do you have your keys?" I helped him out of the truck. Putting his arm over my shoulder, I helped him stumble toward the house.

"Yeah. Pocket."

Fortunately, they were in his jacket pocket, and I fished them out and slid the key into the lock. Everyone filed in past me, and then I bolted the door behind us before helping Alexander to the kitchen. I left him leaning against the counter and got his bottle of whatever it was he had in the fridge. He nodded gratefully, and I left him alone with it, quickly checking the other locks before joining everyone in the living room.

Eyes went wide when they looked at me in the light. "What?"

"Find a mirror, Meg," Steph said.

I let myself into the downstairs bathroom and flipped on the light, blinking in surprise. I could understand why they had been staring. My shirt was shredded and soaked in blood–some of it mine, some of it the creature's. Claws and chains had torn my arm, making it raw and bloody. Bruises turned my hand purple, though it had mostly healed, and Fae blood splattered my face. My hair, a wild mess, was really the most reasonable part of me. I glanced down. One of my pant legs was also badly ripped. I turned on the water, wanting to at least get the blood off my face. I tried to straighten my hair, but it was a lost cause without some de-tangler.

"You still look like hell," Gary said when I came back a short time later.

"Thanks."

Alexander looked better. He crouched next to Ann, his eyes shut, a hand on her forehead. I joined him.

After a moment, he looked up. "Do you think you can kill him?"

"I didn't think you wanted me to."

"No, I want you to, but my family won't. I don't think she'll wake up unless he's dead, and my family won't care. If they get him, they'll keep him locked up, but alive. Killing a Sidhe is not a small thing, even one as evil as he is."

I shut my eyes. He had mentioned repercussions before, but to save my friend, I'd do anything I could.

"Yeah, I can kill him."

Chapter 24

"Megan," John protested.

I glared at him. "Really, you're going to have to deal. We'll explain later. We don't have time right now."

John met my glare with one of his own, and I almost felt bad for him, but he looked away first.

"Okay. Alexander, what do we need to do before this guy shows up?"

He shook his head. "The house itself is completely warded. He shouldn't be able to get in. We'll have to meet him outside to fight him." Alexander cast a wary eye around his house. "I hope."

"We need a plan. Can you hide one of us from him?"

Alexander nodded. "I think so."

"All right. We know he wants me. I go outside to wait for him, and you hide Gage with his shotgun somewhere close by. When he comes to try and kill me, we surprise him." Planning ambushes were really not my strong suit.

"What about the rest of us?" Gary asked while Alexander considered my plan.

"Stay inside and be safe."

"We want to help, too."

"The fewer people I have to worry about, the better."

"I think that could work," Alexander said before Gary could protest. "With some minor modifications. Meg, have you figured out how to form claws yet?"

"Uh, I can have claws?"

"Yeah, and I'll take that as a no. Come on."

I followed Alexander into his kitchen, leaving behind a very confused brother and several unhappy friends.

An hour later, I had figured out how to turn my fingers into vicious claws, though it had taken several panicked minutes before I could get them to turn back to normal–while Alexander gave me crap about it.

Finally, I threatened to test their sharpness on him, and he shut up. Now, I stood outside with him, his back pressed to mine, so I wouldn't be surprised from behind. Gage had hidden, though they hadn't told me where. John also stood outside, armed with several knives. Gary and Tad were in the house, and supposed to help keep Steph and Ann safe if the creature should get inside.

The lights were out; the only illumination came from a street lamp that filtered light through the trees and the light reflected from the overcast sky.

It started to snow. I stared at the fluffy, white flakes. The temperature dropped rapidly, causing my breath to frost. I stiffened and could feel Alexander tense behind me. I had my senses as open as I could, using my ability to see heat to try and give me a warning.

The creature's laugh hissed around us like a foul wind.

"Clever vampire thinks she can hunt me?" It laughed again. "Didn't learn the first time. And neither did the half-blood."

"All talk, no action." I tried to sound bored, not sure I succeeded in keeping the paralyzing fear out of my voice.

I had a whisper of warning before it appeared next to us. I shoved Alexander backward and took the brunt of the creature's attack, lashing out with my own claws and raking them through fabric and across ribs. The creature howled and backed away.

"Little vampire has bite." It laughed, and then it attacked us again, flinging Alexander away before I could stop it and digging claws into my shoulders. I cried out in pain and kicked at his overly short shins.

Bones crunched, and the creature snarled, slamming me into a tree. Stars exploded into my vision, blinding me as my head impacted with the solid trunk. Fortunately, there were no low branches.

Alexander had filled me in on that part of the vampire myth. Stakes to the heart might not always kill me, but they would immobilize me. Either way, it would be bad. I staggered, trying to regain my balance. My vision cleared, the creature's Neanderthal face appeared close to my own.

It grinned.

I cried out as it dug its claws into my gut, ripping at flesh, my ribcage starting to give way.

A shotgun roared, and the creature screamed, dropping me to the ground. I lay there, curled up around my abused midsection, red tears of pain leaking from my eyes.

I couldn't do this, couldn't defeat it. The Unseelie was just too strong. The shotgun roared again, but the creature had vanished. My wound began healing, but I could feel my hunger growing stronger as I used energy to close the severe wound. Someone put their hand on my shoulder, and I had to fight myself not to go after him.

"Meg, you're hurt!" John's voice was steady despite the concern and fear I could sense from him.

"I'll be all right." I forced myself to get to my knees. Forced myself to stand, and wavered.

John put a steadying hand on my shoulder. "You're not okay."

"I will be though. Come on. Need to find Alexander."

"Meg."

I pulled away from him, staggering a little as I did so. He followed me closely. I found Alexander lying on the ground, eyes open, but not really focused on anything.

"Hey, Faerie boy," I whispered.

He tried to focus on me and managed to groan. His arm had twisted at an unnatural angle, and it seemed dislocated. His forearm was clearly broken, bent where there was no joint.

"This is going to hurt, but I'm going to get you inside."

He nodded. I touched his arm hesitantly, not completely sure the Unseelie wasn't using some sort of magic to get me to take him inside instead, but it was Alexander. Our link was still there–barely–and I could tell it was him. It hurt me as well as him, but I managed to lift him from the ground and carry him to the house. John opened the door and followed me inside.

Gary asked, "What happened?"

"He got tossed into a tree and doesn't bounce as well as I do." I set him down on the counter.

"Where is Gage?" I couldn't sense his presence.

"Still outside." Gary frowned, voice grim.

"Damn it." I did not want to go back out there, but I wasn't leaving him behind.

I ran out the front door, closing it behind me and hoping they would have sense enough to stay inside. We needed more help, though I didn't know how we were going to get it. We were done for the night. I spotted Gage crouched in a thicker strand of trees, his heat signature standing out brilliantly against the cold air.

I ran over to him carefully, not wanting to get shot.

"Meg?"

"Yeah."

I was close enough to see his eyes go wide. He swung up the shotgun. I ducked, not wanting it pointed at my face. Strong hands gripped me, teeth digging into my shoulder. I screamed, unable to get out of Gage's way. The world faded around me.

I screamed again, and that convinced me I wasn't unconscious. Pain rippled through my shoulder as the creature tore into it. Claws dug into my ribs, and I felt my strength rapidly leave. I panicked, flailing, fighting as best I could against the creature that had latched on like a leach.

The world reformed around me. The creature had carried me a short distance away from the house. I could hear Gage yelling my name. I kicked off a tree in front of me, slamming the creature back into a pine.

Momentarily stunned, it released me enough that I could get out of its grip. The Unseelie grinned, my blood coating its face, feral light glinting in its dark eyes.

"When I'm done with you, little vampire, I'm going to have your friends." It laughed, and I had no doubt that it told the truth.

Something inside me snapped. I snarled, letting instinct I didn't know I had take over, and managed to duck his next lunge.

Surprised, the creature overshot me, and I leapt onto its back, sinking my teeth into its throat, catching the big vein. Blood flowed freely, and I drank some of it as I sank my claws into the thing's ribcage as it had done to me. I wrapped my legs around him and squeezed, hearing things snap.

It howled. I drank, feeling its energy flag as mine strengthened. It wasn't enough though. I couldn't kill him like this. I slipped one hand free of his ribcage and reached to my side, clutching the knife that had to be burning him through his clothes, pressed between us as it was.

The Unseelie screamed again, fighting to be free of me. It slammed me into a tree, but I kept my hold on it and the knife. Praying I wouldn't miss, I gripped the knife backward and dug it into the creature's sternum.

Its cry split the night, piercing me to the bone, shattering my eardrums, shaking the trees around us. It screamed, and I drank its life as it tried to escape me. I twisted the knife, hunting for its heart, finding it, jerking the knife through the creature's body.

It finally flung me off, just as I felt its life force flee. Afraid it would escape even then, I grabbed for the fleeing spirit, and–not knowing how I did it or what I even attempted–I captured it, channeling it into the ground, because I didn't know what else to do. Energy surged through me, taking the last of my strength, and I collapsed. The Unseelie was dead. That was all that mattered.

I lay on the ground, not willing to move. Everything hurt all the way down to my soul. Monster. The word echoed in my head.

I'd killed something. I hadn't wanted to, but at the same time, a part of me had relished in the kill, reveled in feeling its life fade. I felt sick. The creature's blood filled me, and I used the energy it gave me to start to heal my many injuries, but I couldn't bring myself to move from the ground. Even when Gage called my name.

Alexander's earlier thought echoed through my head again. Maybe it would be better if you didn't go home.

They found me later. Strong arms lifted me, cradling me. I had no idea who carried me, and I didn't care. I wanted to sleep forever. A voice in the back of my head whispered that it was an option, and I had a hard time ignoring it.

They set me on Alexander's counter again. It felt cool and hard under my abused body.

"Will she survive?" I heard Steph ask as if through a tunnel. "Oh, God, she looks horrible."

"I don't know," Gage muttered. "Hard to tell, though I'm guessing most of the blood isn't hers."

I tried to make myself talk, to reassure them, but I couldn't. It was too much work.

"I'd let her rest." Alexander's voice cracked with pain.

"You both need a hospital," John protested.

"John, everything is fine. Go lay down," Alexander whispered. My brother's presence left the kitchen.

"Will she be okay?" Ann's voice set me at ease. She was alive. I'd succeeded. I could rest.

I let blackness claim me, not too terribly concerned if I woke or not.

Chapter 25

I finally did wake, not because I wanted to, but because I couldn't stay asleep any longer. I had a vague sense that if I allowed myself to continue to sleep I wouldn't wake up, and as sick at heart as I felt, I couldn't bring myself to do that. My body ached when I moved, in a dull, healing sort of way. I suspected I'd feel fine before too long.

I was still at Alexander's house, in the soft, white bed I'd slept in before. It was dark outside. I could sense the night, more strongly than normal, and I could hear voices from downstairs. Everyone was still there, which surprised me. Well, not everyone. I couldn't sense John. As before, there were fresh clothes on the end of the bed. I quickly showered and dressed, not quite wanting to face my friends, but knowing I had to. I went silently down the stairs and hesitated in the entryway to the living room, surprised at what I saw.

Sleeping bags, five of them, were strewn on the floor. The remnants of popcorn filled a large glass bowl, and it surprised me that I hadn't smelled it earlier. It looked like a large slumber party.

"Meg!" Steph saw me first, as she sat curled up on the smaller couch with Gary across from where I stood in the doorway.

I smiled a little, the warm welcome making me feel better.

"You had us worried." Gary grinned at me.

"Sorry."

Ann sat on the bigger couch with Alexander, who looked pale, but obviously alive. His arm was wrapped in a crude splint, and white bandages peeked out from underneath his shirt. Tad and Gage were sitting in the two armchairs.

"Did I miss a party?"

"Look outside," Gage said.

Confused, I walked to the nearest window, feeling the cold even with the curtain pulled shut. I opened it slowly and stared, surprised. A blanket of white outside blocked out even the nearest trees.

"I took your brother home and fixed his memory and your mom's. We got back right before the snow really hit. It is officially a blizzard outside," Alexander explained.

"How long have I been unconscious?"

"It's only the next evening."

"Gage says you killed the Unseelie?" Alexander didn't seem quite sure he wanted the answer.

"Yeah." I wasn't interested in going into details.

"Are you sure?"

"I shoved a knife into his chest and drank his life. Yes, I'm sure," I growled. "I felt his spirit flee and channeled it into the ground."

My friends stared. I wondered if perhaps they were reconsidering being happy to see me.

"Oh." Alexander broke the tense silence after a moment. "He's dead then. Really dead. It can be hard to tell sometimes."

I shut my eyes, trying to quell my anger. It wasn't Alexander's fault, not really.

If I was truly being honest with myself, it was my fault. The creature had come here, because it liked feeding from fresh vampire victims, live ones, and I didn't kill my prey. I wasn't sure if that was normal or not, but he had obviously been attracted to me and my friends because of my actions.

Tad touched my shoulder, surprising me. He stepped back when I looked up sharply, but he smiled and held out his hand.

"Come on. We were going to watch bad horror movies."

"Really?" That seemed too cliché to even contemplate.

Tad grinned, taking my hand when I didn't take his, and tugged me toward the rest of my friends.

I ended up squeezed between Ann and Tad on the couch. They had indeed chosen bad horror movies–*Army of Darkness* to be exact.

Alexander gave me an envious look when I sat.

"What?"

"I wish I healed as fast as you did."

I snorted. "It has a high cost."

He shrugged. "Most things do."

I thought about that for a while as the movie started, though Bruce Campbell and his boom stick finally distracted me, and I let myself be pulled into the bad animation and shaky story that nevertheless was fun to watch with friends.

Ann leaned over during part of the movie. "Thank you," she whispered.

"For what?"

"Alexander told me what you did to save me. You could have been killed. You had to kill something. Thank you."

I hadn't quite thought of it like that. "You're my friend. Of course I saved you."

Ann smiled.

A bit of warmth started in my core. I had saved her. I'd saved lives like I wanted to, and even the good guys had to kill people every once in a while. I felt a smile tugging at the corners of my mouth. Maybe I could still be some sort of hero, just not the kind I had thought.

Tad put his arm around me and squeezed gently, obviously hearing, though he didn't say anything.

I stiffened in surprise, but after a moment relaxed, enjoying being held.

The storm abated the next day, which was good because I began to feel uncomfortably hungry again. The Unseelie's life had sustained me longer than normal, but even that didn't last forever. But we were able to go home, and the temporary break from reality had been welcome.

Alexander had done a good job of altering Mom's memory, as well as John's, and neither of them seemed to think anything unusual had occurred. I was extremely grateful. I figured I had saved his life more times than he'd saved mine recently, so I didn't think I would end up owing him anything out of this.

I still wasn't sure why I was so concerned about owing Alexander, but in all the stories I recalled reading, being in debt to the Fae never ended well. I put my worries out of mind and managed to finish up the last bit of homework I had before the winter break. It felt strange to go back to normal things like school and hunting. Sad that hunting was normal. It was equally shocking that the fall semester was almost over.

There was still a lot of snow on the ground, but the sky was overcast the next morning, and the Jeep was up to the task, so I headed to school like nothing out of the ordinary had ever occurred.

Where, of course, the talk of the day was the winter dance. I tried not to be grumpy when people talked about it, jealous that my friends were both going, but I'd already decided not to ask John.

I could go alone, but that would be a little too much for me.

"Meg, what's wrong?" Steph finally asked at lunch while I tried not to sulk in a corner as she and Ann chatted happily about the dance the following night.

I shook my head. "I'm fine. Just having a hard time coming back to reality, I guess."

Steph nodded, but I could sense she didn't believe me.

"Ask Tad to go to the dance," Ann said. Apparently everyone knew what was wrong.

"Um, I can't take someone to a dance."

"Why not?"

"Well, because." I didn't want to say aloud my reason, especially in school. I couldn't take someone, because I was a vampire. I killed things. I didn't go to dances. "Besides, Tad doesn't want to go to a dance with me. He's older than I am and not a high school student and, well..." I'm a vampire, and he knows it, I thought.

"How do you know he doesn't want to go? Have you asked him?" Steph's words were reasonable, but I ignored them.

"Of course I haven't asked him. I'd be surprised if he even likes me. Why would he?"

"Hmm...because you're kind of cool, and you saved all of our lives, and well, he hasn't indicated that he doesn't like you."

"It's not going to happen."

Steph sighed. "Fine, don't ask him. I will. But don't mope around either."

"But you're going with Gary."

"Not for me, silly."

She pulled out her phone.

"Um, no. Don't, please." I was surprised at how desperate I sounded. "Really don't."

"Why? You sound afraid, Meg. What's there to be afraid of? You already defeated the evil Unseelie. Tad is nice.

He likes you, and I'm sure he'd love to go to the dance with you." She did put her phone away though.

"I'm not afraid. I just don't think it's a good idea."

I could tell she wanted to press the issue, but the bell rang, and I used the excuse to jump up from the table, not quite vampire quick, and flee.

Steph didn't bring the subject up again when I gave them a ride home from school, and I was grateful. I wasn't sure if I could take it right now. I felt bad enough that I might just stay home sick Friday and start my vacation early.

I was so grumpy I didn't notice the house was empty until I made it halfway up the stairs to my bedroom. I stopped, shocked, and stretched out my senses, but I smelled no blood, no sense of struggle, and most importantly, Mom's car wasn't in the garage. They'd probably gone shopping.

I took a deep breath and calmed myself. The Unseelie was dead. I didn't know what had me so jumpy now. I forced myself the rest of the way up the stairs and tossed my backpack on my bed before surveying my room.

It seemed to belong to someone else. A handful of books on a small shelf littered with the memorabilia of eighteen-some-odd years of life. There were papers from school scattered on a desk, my dusty lamp, and frilly pillows and curtains left over from a younger me–a phase I'd never been able to escape, even after I'd grown out of it.

None of it was my world anymore.

A world of blood, of death, all cloaked under the darkness of night, of altered memories and stolen time. It seemed that, perhaps, I wasn't supposed to have survived the attack that night. Sure, I had saved lives, but others had died because of me. What did that mean for me? I had never given much thought to a soul and what happened after I died. I was raised generally Christian, but, especially after my father had died when I was seven, Mom hadn't held much with religion. I had no illusion that I would live forever. Something would catch up to me eventually, and then what? Was there a hell reserved for vampires?

I sank onto my soft bed and flopped back into the comforter. What next? Hell, I didn't even know how I would get through the rest of high school. College might be out of the question.

The trill of my cell phone startled me. "Hello?"

"Meg, it's Alexander. Can I talk to you for a sec?"

"Sure."

"My family is going to want to talk to you."

"Okay. When?" My stomach sank, and I shivered at that thought.

"I'm not sure, but I wanted to warn you. They aren't pleased, but I think it will be all right."

"Thank you for making my afternoon so much better." I snarled.

"I have to leave after the dance, and I wanted to make sure I had a chance to talk to you. I think I can smooth things out, but keep your eyes open."

"For what?"

"I don't know." I could hear the frustration in his voice.

"Great."

"I'm sorry." He really did sound sorry. "I'll talk to you later, Meg. And for what it's worth, thanks."

"Sure. Bye." I ended the call and stared at my phone. Damn.

I sighed and suddenly the house was too empty. I couldn't take the gentle rush of air as the heater kicked on or the empty sounds a house made, echoing around me. I grabbed my coat for appearance's sake, jotted a quick note on a piece of torn notebook paper, and headed back downstairs.

Went for a walk. I'll be back–Meg

I set it on the counter and left the tomb-like quiet of the house.

It felt still outside–the snow from the recent blizzard deadening the sound. I could hear the scattered cars on the distant highway, one every few minutes, but it was muffled, as if I had cotton in my ears. It lent to the sense of unreality that crept over me.

I started to run, giving in to the urge that had filled me for several nights. I gave myself to the twilight, blending with it as I let it carry me.

Predictably, my instincts led me toward my normal food supply. It was too early to sulk in the back booth at the bar, so I went farther, wanting to have life around me, to try and get at least a small sense of reality back.

I headed for campus. There had to be a people there.

Chapter 26

Of course, I hadn't taken into account the winter break. Apparently, it started earlier for the college, and campus was mostly dead. I sighed at my failure and started walking aimlessly before finally finding a stone bench in a small alcove by the library. The seat was cold when I sat on it, but it didn't bother me, so I crossed my legs and stared at the quiet campus.

Now and again, a voice drifted across the air, laughter, or a happy shout as the few students who were still present moved through the snow-filled landscape. I sat silently for a while, losing track of time, just listening to the ebb and flow of the campus. I wasn't sure how long I sat there before I became aware of three very familiar presences coming in my general direction. I tensed, debating leaving, but then wondered why. There was a fair chance they wouldn't even notice me as I skulked there on the stone bench.

Gary, Tad, and Gage walked into view, joking softly with each other in an easy companionship I envied. I felt I had lost some of that with Steph and Ann recently, and I wasn't sure if I'd be able to get it back.

It looked like they would pass me by when Gage glanced in my direction. He stopped, cocking his head to one side before smiling and waving. Gary and Tad gave him a quick look before following his gaze.

I smiled, despite my depression, and waved back, but stayed where I was. I wasn't trying to interrupt.

Gage nudged Tad, almost knocking him over.

"Go talk to her." He spoke quietly, but I could hear.

That confused me, but Steph's words came back. He likes you.

Yeah, right, I thought, though a small worm of hope wriggled into my mind as Gary and Gage both waved again and walked on while Tad headed over in my direction.

"Hey," he said when he got close enough for a human to hold a conversation.

"Hi." I tried to sound happier than I was.

We stared at each other.

"I–"

"We–" Tad said as I started to speak.

We both laughed.

"Go ahead." Tad gestured with his gloved hand.

"I was out walking," I said after a moment. "I thought there would be more people here."

He paused for a minute, and I could see him wondering if I had been hunting. I felt my smile fade, and I dropped my gaze from his face to the ground.

"Can I join you?"

"Sure. Bench is cold."

He shrugged and sat next to me, a little closer than I had expected. He smelled warm, tasty...

I almost got up and left, but I didn't want to hurt his feelings, so I gritted my teeth and ignored my hunger.

"I don't want to interrupt..."

Tad shook his head. "We were headed to the library."

I looked at him and arched an eyebrow. That sounded like an excuse.

"No, really, we were." He grinned, and I could sense his sincerity. "We had other plans, too, but we wanted to do some research. They can survive without me for a few minutes. Gary and Gage are actually literate, surprising as that is."

I giggled. Tad had a nice smile.

"Are you doing okay?" He asked after another awkward silence. He didn't clarify, but I knew what he meant.

I shrugged. "Sometimes. I really don't know what I'm going to do."

He nodded. "Yeah. I don't have the problems you do, and I don't know what I'm going to do half the time. I can imagine it being a bit harder for you. I didn't want to interrupt you either. I just wanted to say hi."

"I'm glad you did."

He nodded and stood. "I'm sure we'll see each other again." He smiled. "Especially since Steph and Gary seem to be rather smitten with each other."

I rolled my eyes. "Yeah. Poor Gary, getting dragged to a high school dance because of it, too."

"I'm sure he doesn't mind at all."

"Yeah, probably not." I sighed and looked down again.

"You aren't going?" Tad sounded surprised.

"Naw. Certainly not dating anyone now. I wasn't before, but, yeah..."

"Makes sense."

He sounded happy, and I looked up at him again. He still stood there, looking like he really wasn't in a hurry to go anywhere.

"Do you want to go?" I asked before I even realized what I was doing. I snapped my mouth shut and blushed. Shit. "Um, with me, I guess?" I added, in case I hadn't been painfully clear before.

Tad hesitated, and I glanced down again, cursing myself for asking. No, he did not want to go to a stupid high school dance with me.

"Sure."

I frowned, still staring at the snow, not quite sure I'd heard him right.

"Meg?"

"Yeah?" I couldn't bring myself to look up at him.

Tad knelt in the snow in front of me. "Are you okay?"

"I suppose if you keep having to ask me that, I'm not."

Tad reached up and tilted my chin with his finger. I was shocked as his warm skin touched mine. I hadn't noticed him take off his glove.

He reached up and brushed tears from my eyes. I hadn't noticed the warm tracks of bloody tears that trailed down my cheeks either.

I tried to hide my face and my tears, but he wouldn't let me.

"Meg, it's okay. Really."

I tried to smile. "I'm kind of a mess. Maybe you–"

"Shh," he cut me off. "None of that. I know what you are, and I'd like to think I know who you are. It's fine. And I can understand you being a bit of a mess. I think most people would be." He put a hand on my arm. "Even Gage likes you, you know. You have friends."

I blinked, vision blurring for a minute.

"We can help you. I know we can't know what you are going through, but we're here if you need us."

"Ahh."

He frowned, as if sensing how his words could be taken.

"And I'm not saying yes to going to a dance with you because I'm your friend, and I think you need me to. I'm going, because I want to go with you."

"I think I'm a wreck."

Tad laughed and sat back on the bench, putting his arm around me. He squeezed, and I drank in his warmth, his life, and vitality.

"That's okay."

I let him hold me for a while before he started to shiver.

"Okay, you're cold, and you need to get inside. We can't go to the dance together if you're in bed sick."

"Yes, ma'am." He grinned again, standing. "Can I pick you up tomorrow night?"

I frowned at him.

"I know you normally drive and all..."

"Oh. Uh, sure. You remember where I live?"

Tad nodded.

"Do you have a car?"

Tad laughed. "Yes. Both Gary and I have cars, but Gage prefers to drive, and his truck is bigger than either of our cars, so we let him."

I smiled. "Cool. I'll see you tomorrow night then. Um...we can skip dinner, though."

Tad smiled. "It's a deal."

He squeezed my shoulder, then left. I watched him walk away, not really sure what to think. He turned and waved before he walked out of my view, but I followed him with my senses until he was inside the library and relatively safe.

It didn't dawn on me until I got home that I had another problem. I had nothing to wear. I hadn't gone to the homecoming dance this year. We'd had a sleepover instead, so I couldn't reuse a dress I didn't have. I had some nice clothes, but nothing formal.

I'd also have to tell my mom. Maybe I should have just kept my mouth shut. John and Mom were in the kitchen when I let myself back in the front door.

"Hey, guys," I called.

Mom turned and gave me a smile. "Hi, Meg. You look happy. What's up?"

"Uh." I didn't know what to say, so I decided for the truth. "I asked a boy I like to the dance." Then I frowned. "But I don't have a dress."

John smiled at me. "This is a nice boy, right?"

I nodded. "Tad." I wasn't sure how much John remembered, but he seemed to recognize the name.

"Gary's friend?"

"Yeah."

"I suppose I can allow that."

I snorted. "I see."

"If you don't mind an older style, I might have a dress you can wear," Mom said. "It's upstairs and might not be any good. We will find something, though."

She sounded really happy, and that kind of confused me, but I let it go. I wasn't about to pretend to understand anything right now. I was still too confused myself.

The dress wasn't damaged, and it fit, so I found myself staring in the mirror, hardly recognizing myself, the following evening. The dress was black and off the shoulder, with a tight bodice covered with looser fabric that bunched attractively. It clung to my waist and hips and flared out in a skirt that flowed as I moved. Mom had done my hair, and it sat piled on top of my head. I didn't look like me. The girl in the mirror had more curves than I'd ever possessed and stared back at me, as if asking who inhabited her body, borrowing it for a night as it were.

The doorbell rang. I didn't answer, still staring in shock. Still not quite convinced the mirror wasn't an illusion. Still not convinced Tad would show up, even after my mom called up the stairs to tell me he was there.

Finally, I forced myself away from the mirror and down the stairs.

Shoes had been a little bit of an issue. My feet were not the same size as my mom's–not even close enough to fudge it for a while. That had required a last-minute shopping trip, but the heels I now wore actually matched and gave me a couple of extra inches in height.

If I hadn't had my new vampire abilities, I wasn't sure I would have been able to walk in them.

As it was, if I twisted an ankle, I'd heal quickly.

Tad was talking with John and my mom, flowers clutched awkwardly in his hands. His hair was brushed and pulled back into a short ponytail, and he wore a dark suit. It looked good on him.

I smiled, staring from the hallway. As if sensing my gaze, Tad stopped mid-sentence and turned.

His eyebrows went up, and his jaw dropped a little before he visibly forced himself to shut his mouth.

"You look amazing."

I blushed and managed to make it the rest of the way down the stairs without falling or otherwise embarrassing myself.

"I want pictures," Mom declared before I could get Tad out the door.

I rolled my eyes, and he smiled, but we let Mom pose us and snap off photographs.

John gave me a hug and warned Tad to take care of me, and then we were out the door and into the beautiful night.

I even remembered a coat.

Did You Enjoy This Book?

Then please leave a review and
Be sure to check out *Sabaska's Tale* by J.A. Campbell!

To Anna, horses were more than a fascination, they were everything. Luckily, she had the opportunity to spend every summer on her grandmother's horse ranch in Colorado. Life was perfect, until she received the devastating news that her grandmother had been tragically killed. Anna knew she was the only member of her family who could take over the ranch and hopefully find new homes for her grandmother's beloved Arabians.

Anna wasn't alone for long. Her grandmother had hired a local teenage boy to help tend the horses for the summer. Anna didn't stand a chance against Cody's quiet charm and the two rapidly become friends. However, even with the responsibilities of the ranch, Anna quickly discovers the secrets her grandmother had been hiding and a legacy that sends her on an adventure she never thought possible. An adventure in the saddle of a horse that wasn't a horse at all. Sabaska, her grandmother's favorite Arabian, was a Traveler; a magical being that could travel between worlds. With Anna at the reins, they find themselves trapped in a fight against evil with the highest of stakes... Their very survival.

Other Works by J.A. Campbell

Tales of the Travelers
–Sabaska's Tale
–Sabaska's Quest

Doc Vampire Hunting Dog
–The Moths of Miller Place
–Camping Tales

Into the West

Sky Yarns
–Serpent Queen

Clanless Series
–Senior Year Bites
–Summer Break Blues

Brown Ghost Hunting Dog (Appearing in Various Anthologies)
–Brown and the Saloon of Doom
–Brown and the End of the Line
–Brown Goes Full Steam Ahead
–Brown and the Sand Dragon
–Brown vs. the Martians
–Brown Takes to the Skies
–Brown and the Lost Dutchman Mine

Various Short Stories
–Darkness Taken – Dragonthology
–The Baron and the Firebird – Happily Ever Afterlife
–The Martian Menance of 1897 – Science Fiction Trails 11
–The Life – Six Guns Straight From Hell (Written as Dakota Brown)
–Doc Vampire Hunting Dog, Sheep Interrupted – These Vampires Don't Sparkle II

About the Author

Julie has been many things over the last few years, from college student, to bookstore clerk and an over the road trucker. She's worked as a 911 dispatcher and in computer tech support, but through it all she's been a writer and when she's not out riding horses, she can usually be found sitting in front of her computer. She lives in Colorado with her three cats, her vampire-hunting dog Kira, her new horse and Traveler-in training, Triska, and her Irish Sailor. She is the author of many Vampire and Ghost-Hunting Dog stories and the young adult fantasy series Tales of the Travelers. She's a member of the Horror Writers Association and the Dog Writers of America Association and the editor for Steampunk Trails fiction magazine.

Visit the author's website at:
http://writerjacampbell.wordpress.com

www.ingramcontent.com/pod-product-compliance
Lightning Source LLC
LaVergne TN
LVHW050628100826
845148LV00011B/1774
* 9 7 8 0 6 9 2 2 5 6 0 7 7 *